The Castle

in the Sea

Praise for Mardi McConnochie's
The Flooded Earth

"SET 40 YEARS after a flood that ravages most of the earth, this series starter finds two twins on an epic adventure at sea. Will's biggest problem was having his twin, Annalie, across the country at an elite Admiralty school, until strange men show up at the house. With the house ransacked and his father gone, Will is determined to find answers no matter the risk. After a corrupt Admiralty agent shows up at school, Annalie takes off to help her brother set sail on their father's boat. As they chart the treacherous waters to the Moon Islands, the danger they encounter is real; they struggle to outrun Admiralty agents, stay ahead of pirates, and trust each other. McConnochie covers serious topics prevalent today through the journeys of four kids who provide touches of innocence in this gritty world, each with their own tragedies and obstacles that they turn to one another for help overcoming. A bright adventure that touches upon a range of intense themes, from climate change to the refugee crisis."

—*Booklist*

"IT HAS BEEN 40 YEARS since a massive flood devastated the world. Entire economies collapsed and many people tried to find refuge elsewhere. While more affluent communities were rebuilt over time, others, especially those below the new sea level, were written off, left to fend for themselves. The Navy, best equipped to deal with the aftermath of the flood, took emergency control of the government. When Annalie and Will's father, Spinner, goes missing after he is accused of stealing top-secret technology from the Admiralty, the twins set off an a perilous journey to find him. Annalie leaves her Admiralty-run boarding school where she was ostracized by the other children for living in the "slums," to join Will's search for Spinner. Aided by two other children and a talking parrot, the twins must navigate Spinner's ship while evading the Admiralty, pirates, and other dangers. Not sure whom to trust, the children must rely on their own intuition and skill. Originally published in Australia, this adventure novel is a strong series opener with a unique and timely concept. The fast-paced story will keep readers engaged, and solid world building will draw readers into this fascinating cli-fi (climate fiction) tale. A timely addition to most middle grade collections."

—*School Library Journal*

"A HIGH-SEAS ADVENTURE stars 12-year-old twins Will and Annalie, who seek their missing father in a flooded, post-ecological-collapse world. This trilogy opener, first published in Australia as *Quest of the Sunfish* (2016), begins in the slums of a coastal city 40 years after the Flood that reshaped global geography and politics. Will loves sailing and working in the workshop with their dad, Spinner, while Annalie is more bookish and is the first kid from Lowtown with a scholarship to her prestigious school. Neither knows of anything hinky about Spinner, so they're both shocked when Spinner takes off moments before intruders trash the workshop. Annalie, accompanied by Essie, her only school friend, escapes from school and sneaks home to help. It seems as though Spinner's on the run from the Admiralty that rules most of the post-Flood world, and the kids aren't safe. The three children and a cyborg parrot with augmented intelligence set out on the Sunfish to find Spinner. As is typical of the cli-fi genre, McConnochie explores current-world issues within her adventure. Climate refugees and strict immigration laws have created a permanent underclass and a human trafficking problem, which privileged Essie begins to understand when the adventurers are joined by a starving former slave boy. Racial descriptors are few; naming conventions will have readers imagining the principals as mixed-race or Asian. Despite the post-disaster setting, an exciting and old-fashioned sailboat quest with pirates, secret codes, storms, and cannibals."

—*Kirkus Reviews*

The Castle
in the Sea

Mardi McConnochie

pajamapress

First published in Canada and the United States in 2019

Text copyright © 2017 Mardi McConnochie
This edition copyright © 2019 Pajama Press Inc.
Originally published by Allen & Unwin: Crow's Nest, New South Wales, Australia, 2017

10 9 8 7 6 5 4 3 2 1

www.pajamapress.ca info@pajamapress.ca

 Canada Council Conseil des arts
for the Arts du Canada

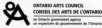 ONTARIO ARTS COUNCIL
CONSEIL DES ARTS DE L'ONTARIO
an Ontario government agency
un organisme du gouvernement de l'Ontario

 Canada

The publisher gratefully acknowledges the support of the Canada Council for the Arts and
the Ontario Arts Council for its publishing program. We acknowledge the financial support
of the Government of Canada through the Canada Book Fund (CBF) for our publishing
activities.

Library and Archives Canada Cataloguing in Publication
McConnochie, Mardi, 1971-, author
    The castle in the sea / Mardi McConnochie.

(The flooded Earth)
Originally published by Allen & Unwin: Crow's Nest, New South Wales,
    Australia, 2017.
ISBN 978-1-77278-083-3 (hardcover)

    I. Title.

PZ7.M47841335Cas 2019   j823'.92   C2018-905922-2

Publisher Cataloging-in-Publication Data (U.S.)
Names: McConnochie, Mardi, 1971-, author.
Title: The Castle in the Sea / Mardi McConnochie.
Description: Toronto, Ontario Canada : Pajama Press, 2018. | Originally published by Allen
    & Unwin, Australia, 2016. | Series: The Flooded Earth Trilogy #2. | Summary: "Twins
    Will and Annalie Wallace continue to search for their missing father. As the Admiralty
    closes in, Will, Annalie, and their friends Essie and Pod must evade capture—and
    pirates—while tracking Spinner's movements around the world in their small sailboat.
    Following a coded list, they make contact with other former scientists living undercover,
    and learn disturbing information about the research their father stole and its connection
    to the global flooding that changed their world"— Provided by publisher.
Identifiers: ISBN 978-1-77278-083-3 (hardcover)
Subjects: LCSH: Twins – Juvenile fiction. | Sailing ships – Juvenile fiction. | Survival at sea
    – Juvenile fiction. | Family secrets – Juvenile fiction. | BISAC: JUVENILE FICTION /
    Science fiction. | JUVENILE FICTION / Action & Adventure / Pirates. | JUVENILE
    FICTION / Dystopian.
Classification: LCC PZ7.M336Ca |DDC [F] – dc23

Cover design by Rebecca Buchanan
Text design based on original by Midland Typesetters, Australia

Manufactured by Friesens
Printed in Canada

Pajama Press Inc.
181 Carlaw Ave., Suite 251, Toronto, Ontario Canada, M4M 2S1

Distributed in Canada by UTP Distribution
5201 Dufferin Street Toronto, Ontario Canada, M3H 5T8

Distributed in the U.S. by Ingram Publisher Services
1 Ingram Blvd. La Vergne, TN 37086, USA

For Annabelle and Lila

The barometer falls

"We've got some weather on the way," Will said. It had been three weeks since Will, Annalie, Essie, Pod, and Graham the parrot had escaped from Little Lang Lang Island. They'd sailed east as fast as they could, fearing that at any moment an Admiralty cruiser would appear over the horizon. Their destination was a remote island, Dasto Puri, on the eastern reaches of the Moon Islands. This, they hoped, was the home of Dan Gari, one of the four scientists who had worked with Spinner on a top-secret research project, and whose name appeared on a coded list written in Spinner's handwriting. This list was their only solid clue to Spinner's possible whereabouts.

For now, the sky was clear and the sun was shining. It didn't seem possible that bad weather was brewing. But the barometer had begun to drop steeply; soon the wind dropped away and the water became a flat, oily slick, all the more disturbing because it seemed so placid. Then the wind began to blow again, a new wind from the south, and it came in hard and fast. The sails began to slam, the rigging to keen. The noise level rose with the wind, an audible warning of what was to come.

"This is going to get bad," Will said. "We have to bring the sails in."

Graham sat on a railing at Will's elbow. "Hate storms," he said. "Hate wet. Bad Will making Graham go to sea."

"Why is it *my* fault?" Will said.

Annalie, Pod, and Essie set to work furling and reefing the sails, but the surging wind made it difficult, and a rising swell made the boat rock and pitch beneath their feet. The storm was coming at them like an express train. A wave broke over the boat, drenching them all, and they grabbed for whatever they could to prevent themselves being washed across the deck.

A huge gust of wind blasted over them. The sails roared, the rigging shrieked, and Will thought he could hear the masts creaking. "Hurry!" he shouted. "This is only going to get worse!"

Annalie, Pod, and Essie managed to get the mainsail furled and reefed. Will was working hard at the wheel to keep the boat with its stern pointed in the direction of the waves—the safest way for it to be pointing—but it kept drifting broadside. He watched with growing frustration as the others struggled, sure that he could do a better job himself, but not trusting any of them to be able to handle the wheel. Annalie paused to give an instruction to Essie, who hurried to do as she was told.

"Where are you going?" Will asked as she passed him.

"Life jackets," Essie said.

The waves were getting bigger, and the *Sunfish* was now climbing up waves that seemed higher than the boat, pausing horribly at the top, and then racing down the face of them and into the trough, the last sail straining in the ever-strengthening winds. If they didn't get it down, they risked damaging the rigging or the mast, or worse, being dragged broadside where the waves could pound the boat, or even roll it.

Annalie was in the bow, struggling to get the foremost sail in, when a huge gust snapped one of the ropes holding it. The sail flew free, almost flinging Annalie with it out of the boat, and then wrapped around the mast. She began to wrestle with it, but the sail, big and sodden, beating in the wind, was almost impossible to disentangle. Gusts of wind kept capturing it, and Will could see it wasn't possible for one person to both furl the sail and disentangle the ropes trailing from it. It was at least a two-person job.

They sailed up the steep face of another wave; as they reached the crest, it broke over the boat, submerging them in a storm of white water. For a moment, Will could see nothing. Then the water drained away and Annalie appeared again, clinging to the railing like a drowned rat.

Essie struggled toward him, holding life jackets and safety harnesses. She was already wearing her own. "Here," she said.

"Spinner doesn't believe in safety harnesses," Will said. His father thought it was a mistake to put your faith in a harness which could fray or break or come unclipped, and which stopped you moving freely around the boat. He'd taught them it was better to trust your own strength and sea legs than to put your faith in a bit of wire.

"Then at least put this on," Essie said, shoving a life jacket at him. "If you don't, Annalie'll kill me." Will shrugged it on.

Pod was now trying to help Annalie with the tangled sail, but neither of them seemed to be making much progress. Will knew Pod was mortally afraid of being washed overboard, and he could see this was preventing him from being much help.

"Pod!" he yelled, his voice tiny in the roar of the wind. "Take the wheel!"

Pod looked back, his face drained by fear. Essie was clambering forward across the pitching deck, clutching more life jackets, to where Annalie still gamely battled. Pod scrambled past her, grabbing a life jacket on the way, and took the wheel.

"Try to keep her stern to the waves," Will shouted.

Pod nodded and gripped the wheel tight. Will knew just how he felt—the boat was being slammed by waves, rocked by the wind, and the rigging was shrieking. It seemed scarcely possible that such a small craft could stay afloat and intact in this world of water. *She's a good boat*, he told himself as he scrambled forward to help Annalie. *She's been through worse. She'll make it through.*

"Get the ropes untangled," he yelled as he reached the girls. "I'll deal with the sail."

The girls tugged at the ropes and Will fought with the sail. Flapping and gusting, it resisted furling, and for a moment the wind caught it and Will felt it almost lift him off his feet. Annalie reached out and grabbed him, and then the two of them hauled in armloads of soaking-wet sail, bunching and scrunching it until it was under control.

"I'll stow it!" Annalie shouted, and began to struggle with the sail toward the nearest empty locker.

"We're done here," Will shouted to Essie over the roar of the storm. "You should go below!"

Essie nodded, and the two of them turned to make their way back to the hatch, but the deck was starting to rear up again beneath their feet as they rode up the back of another huge wave. Will glimpsed Annalie still struggling to stow the sail in a locker on deck as the *Sunfish* reached the crest of the wave. For a moment, they were poised on the top of it, and then they were sliding, rushing down the face, fast, way too fast, the force of the water pushing the boat sideways. Will grabbed onto the railing. Looking back down the boat, he saw Pod frantically turning the wheel, but the rudder wouldn't bite and he couldn't control their motion. Still they slid, down and down the wave; it was breaking right behind them, and suddenly the great foaming wall dropped straight onto the *Sunfish*, burying it once more. This time, Will was knocked loose from the railing. Foam captured him and surrounded him and there was nothing solid to hold onto at all, just water on every side, and then the storm swallowed him.

Man overboard

The *Sunfish* struggled clear of the wave, water streaming from her deck.

Annalie looked down into the locker—it was half-full of seawater, but the sail was finally in there. She latched it shut and looked up, and only then registered what sounded like a cry. She looked around her and saw no one, then looked back and saw only Pod, his mouth wide in a shape of distress. She could barely hear him, but her brain picked up the sense of it: "Man overboard!"

Terror, electric, jolted through her. "Where?" she shrieked back.

Pod pointed and she ran to look over the side.

Gripping the railing, she could see a spot of orange in the water—Essie. She had her life jacket on, but already the storm was driving them apart, so fast, impossibly fast.

She turned back to Pod and shouted, "Where's Will?"

Pod just held his hands up helplessly.

Annalie dashed to the other side of the boat and looked for him, but there was no sign of her brother.

She looked up and saw Graham screeching.

"Graham, where's Will? Can you see him?"

"Graham look!" he said, and took off into the storm. She watched for a brief fearful moment as Graham's strong wings battled the fury of the wind, then she ran back to where Essie was still visible, calling to her for help. She grabbed a life-preserver on a long rope and flung it out, hoping Essie might swim to it, but it fell short. Essie struggled toward it, but made little headway.

"Swim!" Annalie screamed. "Swim!"

But Essie was floundering in the massive storm swell, unable to close the gap.

Annalie hauled the life-preserver back in and threw it again, using all her strength. But the waves were coming between them now, the storm pushing them even farther apart. There was no way Essie could reach it. Annalie took another good look round, hoping to see a second spot of orange—a sign that Will was still on the surface, could still be saved. Nothing. Essie waved desperately, and Annalie's heart twisted in her chest.

She clambered back to the wheelhouse. "I'm going in after her," she said. "I'll tether myself to the boat and you'll have to haul us back in."

"If you go in the water," Pod said, "you drown. You and her both."

"But I have to try!" Annalie shrieked. "I can't just leave her there!"

"You want to drown too?" Pod said. "I can't sail this boat by myself. You jump overboard, we're all dead. You, me, all of us. You stay here, maybe we'll make it."

Annalie stared at him. She knew he was right: even if she could swim out to Essie—unlikely—and manage to get to her without her friend panicking and pushing her under, and even if she could get herself winched back to the boat, in these mountainous seas, how would they ever get back on board without getting battered against the hull? It was an ironclad law of the sea that if someone went overboard, especially in a storm, you did not go in after them. She knew that. But the horror of it—leaving her best friend in the water to drown—was almost unbearable.

"She's got a life jacket on," Pod said. "Maybe she'll be okay."

But neither of them really believed it.

And where was Will? She hadn't seen him, hadn't seen his life jacket. She knew he'd put one on, but what if it was faulty, or hadn't been done up properly, and was torn from him by the massive wave? Was he sinking, even now, to the bottom of the sea? But no, she didn't want to think about it.

She heard a tearing *skrark* from Graham, and the bird half-flew, half-crashed onto the deck, soaking wet and worn out from the wind. "No Will," Graham said. "Will lost."

Annalie looked at him in despair, knowing she couldn't ask Graham to go out for one more pass. She could see he was exhausted.

"What are we going to do?" Pod asked.

Annalie stood there, frozen. She couldn't think.

In one moment, her brother and her best friend had been washed overboard. They had been there, and then they were gone. Lost.

"You know about storms. What do we do?" Pod repeated.

"I don't know," Annalie said. "I don't know."

They began to climb up the face of another wave. This one seemed even bigger than the one that had claimed Will and Essie, the ascent endless, and all the more horrifying because of the thought of what might lie over the front of it. They reached the top; they hung there; and then the boat pitched forward, until it seemed to be almost vertical on the wave, its bowsprit pointing straight at the bottom of the ocean. And then they began to fall. They fell and they fell, the boat accelerating like something out of a nightmare, and then it began slewing around, and another wall of water hit them and they were rolling. Annalie was hurled straight off her feet and the only thing that stopped her being washed into the water after her brother was the lifeline clipped to her life jacket. Unlike Will, Annalie thought there was a time and place for lifelines, and this was one of them. She smashed hard against a railing, and then she was right underwater, bobbing and yanking like a fish on a line, and she thought, *This is it, we're rolling. We're going to roll right over.* But at the last moment, the boat came the right way up again.

Something in the scream of the wind through the rigging made her look up through salt-stung eyes. The main mast had bent and broken—it wasn't snapped off, but it would be useless until they could get it repaired.

Her heart pounding, she turned and saw Pod still clinging to the wheel, wet and terrified, but determined. He was waiting for her to take charge of the situation, to tell him what to do, and the terror of that moment of being afloat underwater, not knowing which way was up and which was down, snapped her back into the present moment. She had to do something to save the boat, or they could founder.

"We're traveling too fast down the waves," she said. The knowledge was coming to her now, calm and certain, from some place in her memory. "We have to do something to slow the boat down. We need a sea anchor."

Giving the boat some extra drag would slow it down and stop it accelerating and surfing down those waves. She scampered aft to where the long, heavy chains were kept, cleated one on, and heaved it overboard. The long chain paid out behind them, and they noticed the difference at once. The boat sat a little lower in the water, and when the next wave lifted them up there was no feeling of lift-off; the extra drag meant the *Sunfish* hugged the water and was no longer being picked up and carried by the waves. The boat, which had seemed to be flying perilously forward with the storm, now seemed to be sitting still, or even going backward. The steering was heavy, and the boat sluggish, but they were no longer losing control of it with every wave that rolled along.

The storm went on for hours. Annalie and Pod

took it in turns to wrestle with the steering. Sleep was impossible; so was eating. Even though the cabin hatches were sealed, water pushed in around the seals whenever a particularly large wave crashed over the decks, so everything was sodden. And any item that had not been carefully stowed before the storm began was now a rolling, smashing, flying menace, tumbling backward and forward around the cabin with every pitch and roll.

Graham screeched and squawked in the early part of the storm, but as the hours wore on he fell silent, clinging grimly to his perch, too tired to do anything but hold on.

At around midnight the storm began to subside, and by the early hours of the morning it had passed over them entirely. Pod, Graham and Annalie, deathly tired, snatched a few hours of dreamless sleep.

Beating into the wind

When they woke later that morning, the sea had changed its face once more, switching from raging, snarling, storming gray to a vast, tranquil green-blue.

Pod, Annalie and Graham sat on deck. Everything below was wet and stinking, streaked with food and fuel and vomit. They'd found a small number of dry biscuits in a container that hadn't smashed, and they made a melancholy breakfast.

"So," Pod said after a while. "Now what?"

Annalie took a moment to finish her biscuit, weighing the question. She looked up at the main mast, splintered and broken about a third of the way up its height, leaning at an angle, the rigging shredded. She looked at the array of solar cells and turbines—many smashed, others missing altogether. She thought about all the stormwater that had forced its way in and wondered if it had fouled the big water storage tanks in the hull. She thought about the food, the tools, the equipment smashed to bits as it rolled around the cabin. Then she thought, *At least we only need to feed two people now.*

And that was where her thoughts stopped. A low, dismal, terrible feeling swept over her and she couldn't think, couldn't begin to see what they should do next. Will and Essie had been swept overboard and lost, and it felt like it was all her fault. Why hadn't she done more to save them? She replayed the scene in her head: Essie in the water, calling to her. Why didn't she go in after her? And why hadn't she tried harder to find Will? She hadn't seen him anywhere, but if she'd looked harder, done something…

"Perhaps," Pod said, "we try and make it straight?"

Distracted from her thoughts, she saw Pod was considering the mast.

"Mast stuffed!" Graham said.

"We can't make it perfect," Pod said, "but maybe we can fix it a bit, so we can put up a sail."

"Look at it," Annalie said. "Graham's right, it's stuffed."

A stubborn look came over Pod's face. "We got tools though, right? Maybe, if we brace it, we can put something up." He paused, waiting for her to take charge. "We can't go and look for them if we don't fix the mast."

Jolted out of her misery, Annalie stared at him. "What?"

"We're going back for them, right?"

Annalie turned to look out at the vast, empty blue stretching away from them on every side. "How would we know where to look?"

Pod frowned, his faith in her wavering. "Can't you look at the charts? Work out where they might've gone?"

Annalie wanted to laugh and cry. Did he think she had magical powers?

"We can't just give up," he said. "You think about it. I'll try and fix the mast."

He got up and went to look for the tools.

Graham sidled over to her and stroked her knee with his head. "Graham help look," he suggested. "Graham has excellent eyesight."

"I know. Thanks, Graham," Annalie said, stroking his feathers. Pod was right: they couldn't give up on Will and Essie. The waters of the archipelago were warm; you could survive in them a reasonably long time, so long as you had something to keep you afloat. And she had a fairly good idea of where they'd been when the storm first hit them—she'd taken their position just a few hours earlier. Surely all she had to do was work out where the *Sunfish* was now, then sail back along the same line. If either of them were still afloat, surely she'd be able to find them.

Filled with a new sense of determination, Annalie jumped to her feet and fetched her charts and instruments. While Pod began straightening the mast, bracing and lashing it with spare oars, bits of timber, rope and wire, Annalie charted a line for their search. The storm had blown them farther off course than she'd imagined, but it was simple enough to note where they'd been, and where they should go looking. Annalie marked up the chart and showed it to Pod.

"This is our search area," she said.

"Okay," Pod said. "That's quite big, right?"

"It is," Annalie said. "But it's hard to be more

specific. How's it all looking?"

"The rigging's a mess, but we can still put up some sail."

"What about the motor?"

"It won't start. Some of the solar panels are smashed, but not all of them, so they should be pulling some juice. But the motor's completely dead."

"Motors were always Spinner's department," Annalie said. "And Will's." Tears threatened; she fought them off. "See what you can do," she said. "In the meantime we'll just have to stick to sail."

Annalie took the wheel and turned the *Sunfish* around, sailing back toward the west. This was not an easy task as the wind was blowing the other way, toward the east, and they were constantly having to tack into the wind to stay on course, which made the patched-up mast creak and groan. Annalie and Pod took turns steering and looking for their missing friends. The sun dazzled off the water, making it hard for them to look for too long without their eyeballs frying. Graham launched himself on mission after mission, flying first to port side, then to starboard, but saw nothing. After lunch, the sail broke loose from the rickety mast and they had to stop to make further repairs. They resumed the search as soon as they could, tacking doggedly into a stiffening breeze. The afternoon wore on. Still they saw nothing. Graham wore himself out flying and had to have a little snooze. The sun began to set.

"Let's stop for the night," Pod said. "We won't be able to see anything soon."

"Let's give it another half an hour," Annalie said, not willing to give up yet.

They kept tacking. No glimpse of fluorescent orange showed itself. When the light was totally gone, Pod appeared again at her elbow.

"Come on," he said. "Let's go below."

They had done nothing to clean up the saloon and it was still just as the storm had left it: wet, messy, littered with spilled and broken things. They had to spend an hour putting it all to rights before they could even sit down to eat.

"Graham fly farther tomorrow," Graham promised.

"We know you're doing your best," Pod said.

"Tomorrow we'll find them," Annalie said.

When the meal was done, she took out her charts and made notes and calculations—distance traveled, distance still to be covered—hoping to find reassurance there. She knew all too well how big the ocean was, and how small one person could be in that great expanse of water. But she had to believe they were still okay. She had to believe she could find them. The alternative was unbearable.

"We've still got a lot of ocean to cover, haven't we?" Pod said.

Annalie nodded.

"This'll be their second night in the water," Pod said.

"It's warm," Annalie reassured him. "They can still make it."

They resumed their search at first light the next

day, beating into the same wind. The sail broke loose again, twice. While Pod was working on the sail for the second time, late in the afternoon, Annalie stood on deck watching Graham come swooping back from one of his searches. Something about the way he bent into the wind gave her an idea she wished she'd had sooner.

Anxiously she checked their position.

Pod came over to her. "How are we doing?"

"If I'm right, we're back to where we were when the storm hit," she said.

"Already?" Pod said, rather surprised. "But... shouldn't we have found them, then?"

"The thing is," Annalie said, "I may not have accounted enough for the wind."

"How do you mean?"

"The wind's blowing this way now," Annalie said, showing him the direction on the chart. "But when the storm came up, it was blowing this way." She showed him the direction of the storm front, which had blown up from the south. "So it's possible when we were traveling from here to here, we weren't going in a straight line, we were going in a curve, because of the strength of the wind gusts."

"Oh," Pod said.

"I mean, I allowed for that. But maybe I didn't allow for it *enough*."

Pod frowned. "So what do we do? Keep going east, or turn back and try going in more of a curve?"

Annalie hesitated, wishing she knew what to do. She didn't know exactly where they'd been when the storm hit, nor did she have any real sense of how far north the storm might have pushed them. And how far had it pushed Will and Essie? So many variables, so much ocean. And she was horribly aware that her brother and her best friend had been in the water for two days now. Even in warm water, that wasn't good.

"For now we keep going," she said. "And if we don't find them, tomorrow we'll turn around and go back the other way on more of a northerly line. Once we're traveling with the wind again, it'll be easier on the mast, and we'll be able to cover more ground that way."

"Okay," Pod said. "I'll take next watch."

They tacked on into the wind until the sun went down. They saw no sign of their lost companions.

The three of them retired to the saloon, gloomy and disheartened. Annalie colored in the chart showing the area that they'd covered that day. It was a solid amount, but still they'd found nothing.

"Tomorrow we'll turn back," Annalie said, marking out the new line, the new search area, studying it for the hundredth time. "I think we just need to go farther north and we'll find them."

Pod nodded. "Okay."

But as she lay in bed that night, all Annalie could think was, *What if we don't find them? What if I've got it wrong? What do we do then?*

At first light the next morning Annalie set the new heading and they sailed on. The sailing was easier now and, despite her night of worry, she felt her spirits rise. *Now we're on the right track*, she told herself. *Today we'll definitely find them.*

But they didn't.

They sailed and searched. Graham swooped and flew. Once, Pod saw a flash of orange far out on the port side, but when Graham went out for a look, he discovered it was just floating sea junk. It was not a life jacket.

The third day ended. Annalie was bewildered, Pod despondent.

"We've looked everywhere I can think to look," Annalie said. "Maybe we missed them somehow."

"I don't know how," Pod said, "we were pretty thorough."

"Maybe tomorrow we start again. Go back to the beginning," Annalie said. "Or start looking in places we haven't already looked."

"Which places?" Pod asked.

They both stared down at the chart with its lines and crosshatches, as if it might suddenly spit out new clues. "I don't know," Annalie said helplessly. The stress and worry of the last three days suddenly rose up in her like a wave, and, to her embarrassment, she started to cry. "I don't know what to do next," she gulped. "We can't just leave them there. But I don't know where else to go."

"Maybe...," Pod said, but couldn't think of anything to suggest either. "You did your best," he said instead.

"My best wasn't good enough," Annalie said.

Graham flew down onto the table and stood on the chart. "Maybe boat find them," he said. "Maybe they're not here. That's why we don't find them." His bright eye glinted at them in the darkness of the saloon.

Pod turned to look at Annalie. "It's possible, isn't it?" he said.

"Anything's *possible*," Annalie said, wiping the tears away.

"If a boat's already picked them up, then we're wasting our time out here," Pod said. "Aren't we?"

"But what if a boat *hasn't* picked them up?" Annalie said.

She remembered the despairing look on Essie's face as she was swept away.

Pod paused. "I checked our water supplies before. The main tank needs to be purged before we can use it again. One of the secondary tanks has got salt in it too. The other one's good, but it's only about half full."

"We're not out of water yet," Annalie said.

"I know," Pod said. "But still."

"Can't search forever," Graham said. "Spinner would say so."

Annalie looked at the wise old bird, and knew he was only trying to help.

Essie, she thought. *Will*. She wasn't ready to give up yet.

"You know, maybe Graham's right," Pod said. "Maybe someone picked them up. For all we know, they could be waiting for us somewhere right now."

"They could be," Annalie conceded.

"Maybe it's time to get help," Pod said. "Raise the alarm. Find out if anybody's seen them."

Annalie let this idea grow in her mind. The thought of getting help came as a welcome relief. "You're right," she said. "We should push on to Dasto Puri and get help there."

Pod looked relieved that she'd come round to his point of view. "Do you think they'll be able to help us?"

"I hope so," Annalie said. "If Dad's friend lives there, there must be *something* there, right? A port, or a town. And he should be able to help us raise the alarm. Send out a search party."

In her mind's eye, she imagined helpful island folk with fishing boats getting on their radios, sending messages, helping them search, discovering Will and Essie miraculously unharmed and hanging out in a little fishing village, waiting to be picked up. Never mind that in most of their previous island encounters the people they met had tried to rob, murder, or eat them; Annalie hoped Dasto Puri would be different.

The Dastos were a young-looking island group, with pointy mountains sticking up from the ocean, many of them clad in a thick blanket of vivid green. One of the largest was topped by a volcano streaming a thin plume of white smoke. In spite of this, people lived here: small boats worked the coastal fringes;

there were settlements in some of the bays, and other buildings, some of them quite large, their purposes unguessable from this distance, farther up the slopes. Annalie felt heartened by all the boats; maybe the local people would know where to look for Will and Essie.

At last they reached Dasto Puri. It loomed threateningly; from a distance it seemed to be all cliffs, and it was hard to imagine that anyone could live there. The surf crashed onto rocks at the base of the cliffs, making landing seem impossible. Light winked from the island, suggesting habitation—glass or metal objects reflecting the sun. As the *Sunfish* drew closer, something came zipping out of the cliffs and sliced through the water toward them.

It was a motorboat, fast and maneuverable, which zoomed toward them and then slewed to a stop. There were three men on board. One was driving; the other two held big guns. Annalie, standing on deck with Pod at the wheel, realized too late that the boat, and the three men on it, were wearing the purple colors she recognized all too well.

"They're Kangs," she said to Pod. "I think Dasto Puri belongs to the Kang Brotherhood."

And the guns were pointed directly at them.

An honest gentleman
of the sea

The Kang Brotherhood was one of the many gangs that flourished where the poorest people of the world congregated: in the slums, like the one Annalie had grown up in; in the refugee camps; in the Moon Islands; and in all those places in their flooded world where too much saltwater had broken governments and ruined people's livelihoods. The Kangs were smugglers, pirates, traffickers, and enforcers, and they were seriously scary people.

The driver of the Kang boat spoke; his voice leaped from an amplified device attached to the front of the boat.

"Where are you headed?"

"Dasto Puri," Annalie shouted.

"What's your business?"

"We've been damaged in a storm," Annalie called. "We need help fixing our boat."

"How many of you are there?"

"Just the two of us," Annalie said.

The driver opened his throttle and the boat took a leisurely turn around the *Sunfish*. The guns remained fixed upon them.

"Okay," the amplified voice said finally. "We'll send someone to tow you in."

Pod looked at Annalie. "You sure this is a good idea?"

"No," Annalie said. "But what choice have we got?"

Soon, a launch appeared and towed them up a treacherously narrow passage between ridged fingers of rock and through a gap in the cliffs that opened onto a deep, handsome bay.

"You know this is a pirate bay, right?" Pod said, looking around him in dismay.

"Yep," Annalie said.

"We just gave ourselves to pirates," Pod said.

"Yep," Annalie said again.

It was a surprisingly busy place, studded with many boats, some of them little and zippy, others bigger and more threatening. Unsurprisingly for a pirate fleet, they all bristled with weaponry.

Pod clutched at his head and said, "I can't believe I'm going back to a pirate bay!"

"It's going to be okay," Annalie said.

"It's *not* going to be okay," Pod said fiercely. "Pirates are bad people. They make you do bad things."

"That won't happen to us."

"Why not? You got money? Lots of money?"

"You know we haven't."

"Then what makes you so special? You want help, you gotta pay. Don't have no money, you might not like what they want you to do."

Annalie frowned. "What do you mean? What do

you think they're going to make us do?"

"I dunno," Pod said. "But bad things. Dangerous things. Things you don't want to do. But if you don't do them, no boat. Or worse."

"What would be worse?"

"You not useful, they sell you. Or just kill you."

"Pirates take our boat?" Graham said. "Turn Graham into barbecue?"

"No one's taking our boat," Annalie said firmly.

"How you planning to stop them?" Pod asked.

They anchored in the bay, and a small boat took them to shore, where a delegation of four Kangs— three men and a woman—waited for them. They were all ostentatiously well-armed.

"Hello there," said the smallest of the three men. Although he was less brawny than the others, it was clear he was their leader: he held himself with a relaxed but confident stance that made it clear he expected to be obeyed. He had no need to threaten them with guns or enormous knives—his bright eyes were intimidating enough. His head was completely shaved and a ferocious tattoo of barbed wire wrapped around his head, complete with tattooed blood droplets. Underneath the tattoo were the ridged lines of real scars; the tattoo had been designed around them, perhaps as a badge of honor. "Looks like you broke your boat."

"We were in a storm," Annalie said. "And two of our friends were washed overboard. We need your help to find them."

The pirate leader pursed his lips. "What did they look like?"

"It was my brother and my friend," Annalie began eagerly. "He's about my height, brown hair—"

She broke off; the pirates were laughing.

The pirate leader smiled smoothly, a tattooed coil of wire contorting on his temple. "They're probably dead," he said coolly. "Which leaves me with the question: What do I do with you?"

Annalie felt a cold, slithering feeling go down her neck. Of course: they would get no help for free.

"We came here because we're looking for someone," she said. "His name's Dan Gari."

"Who?" the pirate leader said with studied indifference.

"He's an old friend of my father's, and I'm pretty sure he lives here. My father's name's Spinner, and he shipped out of Port Fine with one of your crews a little while back, headed for this island."

Although the pirate's expression barely shifted, Annalie knew she had his attention. "Did he, now?"

"I happen to know he paid a lot of money for his passage. There's more where that came from, if you help us."

"Help you with what, exactly?" He ticked it off on his fingers. "Fix your boat. Find this—whatsisname you think lives here. Look for your missing friends. *And* track down your daddy? That's an awful lot of help. And help is expensive."

"I know," Annalie said. "But we're good for it."

The pirate leader studied her for a moment. "What's your name, little girl?"

"Annalie."

"Pleased to meet you, Annalie. My name's Wirehead." He paused, then said, "I don't think you quite understand your situation. I already have you, and I already have your boat. So you're not in a position to ask me for anything." He gave her a genial smile. "But because I'm an honest gentleman of the sea, I'm willing to give you a chance to buy your boat back. If you *are* good for it, as you say, then, all well and good, you can go about your business and we'll see about those other little tasks. If not—well..." He paused, his smile silky but menacing. "That's another conversation."

Wirehead flicked a glance at his associates. "Find them a bunk." Then he turned back to them with a smile. "Welcome to Dasto Puri."

Afloat

Held up only by his life jacket, Will rode the storm for such a long and terrible time that afterward he could not really tell if it had been hours or days. The waves that had seemed impossibly huge from the boat seemed even more vast when he was right down there in the water. Over and over, the waves surged up beneath him, thrusting him upward; over and over, they broke over his head in mountains of fizzing white, and he dropped again, down the face, down and down until it seemed he would plunge right down to the bottom of the ocean. The constant churn was so nauseating that more than once he found himself retching, but it had been ages since he ate; his stomach was empty, and all he produced was bitter acid, which burned his mouth even worse than the salt, leaving him ill and aching. But still his jacket held him up, and although the water kept smashing him in the face, knocking at his mouth and nose and demanding to be let in, somehow he managed to keep the breath in his body and the water out of it, and so the storm did not quite manage to drown him.

Then at last the storm rolled on its way and left him behind.

Will floated, so cold he had stopped shivering long ago. Gray sea around him, gray sky above. No boats, no mountains, no seabirds. Not so much as a hint of land on the horizon, not that he could have swum to it even if he could see it. His limbs were numb. He could barely move them. All he could do was float and keep breathing.

I'm still in the Moon Islands, he thought dazedly. *If I'm lucky, there'll be an island.*

He thought of Pod, thrown overboard by his pirate captain. He had floated on an empty container until he landed on a rock and found rescue. It was the sort of thing that happened in the Islands.

I wonder if Annalie is looking for me, he thought. He told himself that he'd come looking for her if their positions were reversed. *But would I?* he wondered. *She doesn't know if I'm alive. She wouldn't know where to look. She could search for days, or even weeks, and never find me.*

Better face facts, he thought. *There's no way she's coming. I'm on my own.*

And this was such a terrifying thought he could hardly bear it.

Still he floated. He was very thirsty now. Hungry too, probably, but thirst dominated. He could no longer feel his fingers. *If a shark tried to eat me*, he thought, *I'd never feel a thing.*

He slipped into a half-dream, gazing up at the sky, his mind filled with incoherent and disturbing thoughts. Then something crossed his field of vision and snapped him out of it. It was a seagull.

Seagulls don't fly far from shore, he thought. *There must be land nearby.*

Fully awake now, he struggled to move his limbs, to stir himself around in the water, to see if he could see where the bird had come from, and to try and steer himself in that direction. But he could barely signal to his limbs; actually swimming was clearly no longer possible. But somehow he managed to twist himself around, and that's when he saw it: land!

Desperation gave him a fresh burst of energy. *Swim, stupid arms!* he urged himself. *Kick, legs!* Feebly, they stirred. He chose his best survival stroke and struggled on. He had no idea what the land was or what it held, but it was land, and that had to be better than being afloat. He knew he couldn't survive another night in this water.

He swam, with limbs that felt like jelly, trying to get a better view of the island ahead. Through the bobbing waves he could see that it had a few trees on it—green trees—which meant that it had not been completely ruined by salt. It might have fresh water, or food, or maybe even people. But then he noticed something else. The island was moving very fast. When there was only open ocean to look at he had not been aware of it, but now that he had a point of reference, he realized that he must be caught in a current.

If he was not careful, he could be swept right past the island without ever reaching it.

A sob of anguish burst from his throat and he struck out again, willing some strength into his arms. He could not let himself be swept away, he simply could not.

Of course he remembered now that one of the hazards of archipelago sailing was the currents. The islands didn't have to be all that close together to have powerful currents and tides running between them.

Will struggled on, his arms dragging, but the current was too strong. It pulled him carelessly along the length of the island as if he were just another piece of kelp ripped up in a storm. The trees sailed away from him. He could see the end of the island approaching.

He swam—

He swam—

He passed the end of the island.

The current dragged him on. The island receded into the distance. He had missed it.

Despair flooded in, and with it, exhaustion. He slipped into darkness.

Ashore

Will woke suddenly, surprised into semi-conscious- ness by pain.

But it was a pain that only registered dully. Some- thing was rasping against his legs. He peeled open his eyes just as a wave broke over his face. Again, that rasping, scraping feeling.

He had landed on something. Rocks. Gritty sand.

He looked around him, dazedly taking in his surroundings. The current had deposited him in a cove—more of a rocky elbow, really, but a sort of cove.

He was in shallow water. His legs were dragging across the rocky bottom—that was the painful raspy feeling. He got himself to his feet and staggered up out of the water, stumbling and sliding over the rocks, until he was safe on dry land.

Slumping back on the sand, he took stock of where he was. By some miracle, he had washed ashore on an island in a long, narrow inlet. But perhaps it was not such a miracle: he saw that he had washed up in a kind of sea trap that caught vast quantities of the junk that circled the oceans of the world: bits of old rope, buoys and nets, a million broken things. But there were things that might be useful too: he saw plastic sheeting, long spars of timber, some quite big containers which would come in handy to catch rainwater.

Water. He needed water. Right now.

Will heaved himself upright, shucking off his life jacket with fingers that trembled. He crossed the sand and began to look through some of the heaped piles of stuff, focusing his attention on the junk that was higher than the tideline, hoping some upturned container might hold some precious rainwater left over from the storm. He got lucky; he found some that did not taste too funny, and it went down so fast it barely touched the sides. He looked around for more, and that's when he saw it.

Something orange. A familiar shade of orange. A life jacket. And there was something in the life jacket—a shape, sodden, with long wet hair, tangled in debris.

Essie.

His heart almost stopped. She wasn't moving, and the gentle shore break was sluicing over her in a way that filled him with dread. He crept down to her, picking his way through the shifting junk, afraid of what he might find.

He turned her over, lifting the wet, clinging hair from her face. Was she unconscious, or dead? Her skin was wet and cool, and he feared he had found her too late. He put a hand on her neck and couldn't feel a pulse, but he could hardly feel his own hands. He put his head beside her mouth and thought he felt a faint stir of breath. He put his head to her chest.

The waves were loud, but he could sense the knock of her heart, still beating. She was alive!

He disentangled her from the branches and ropes and plastic crap, then dragged her up onto the shore.

"Hey, Essie, can you hear me?" he said, hoping his voice might wake her.

It didn't. He wanted desperately to help her but didn't know where to start. He squatted beside her, trying to think of the most useful thing to do next. Go and look for help? Find water? Build a shelter?

His eyes returned to the epic tangle of debris piled up at the narrow end of the inlet. It was enormous; almost geological. He thought that if anyone actually lived here, they would surely have picked it over for treasure. At a glance he could see valuable objects just sitting there, waiting to be removed. Instinct told him this island was uninhabited.

Water, then. He needed to find more water. And build a shelter.

Then, hopefully, she would wake. And they would think about what they were going to do next.

Castaways

E ssie wandered back into consciousness, queasy, groggy, sandy, and devastatingly tired.

She could hear the gentle wash of waves. Above her, something blue. Pinpricks of sunlight peeked through. It rustled and flapped. A plastic tarp.

She sat up, confused and frightened. She had no idea where she was or how she had come to be here. But where was here?

She heard a shout and saw a figure running up the beach toward her, outlined against the sun-dazzle. She froze—people who ran at you on islands usually had bad intentions—but then her brain caught up with her eyes and she recognized Will.

He flopped down beside her, grinning madly. "You're awake!"

"Where are we?" she asked. Her voice was salt-scoured.

"I dunno. Some island. What are the chances, huh?"

It was all coming back to her. The storm. The waves. She had been swept off the *Sunfish* and into the open ocean. "Why aren't we dead?"

35

"Life jackets," Will said, "and luck." He picked up a plastic container sitting next to her and held it out. "Here. Bet you're thirsty."

She drank it all down in a few gulps, then realized. "Oh. Should I have been rationing that?"

"It's okay," Will said. "I know how to make more."

If she'd been listening, this would have struck Essie as surprising. But she was not really listening. "Where *are* we?" she asked again.

"I dunno."

"You must have some idea."

"I don't carry a map around in my head," Will said.

"So, we're lost?"

"Yeah, I guess so."

Panic was rising up in Essie. "So how will the others know where to come look for us?"

"The others?"

"Annalie. Pod. They're going to come and look for us, aren't they?"

Will scowled. "I wouldn't count on it."

"But they have to. They wouldn't just abandon us."

"They probably think we're dead," Will said. "If I were them, I'd assume we were goners. And you know," he continued, "there's no way of knowing whether they even made it themselves. If they lost control and a wave got them—"

He didn't finish the thought, but it had brought back for both of them the memories, terribly fresh, of the boat plunging and skidding down near-vertical drops, harassed by waves taller than buildings.

Essie stared out at the sunshine sparkling on the water, feeling lost and alone. The ocean had never seemed so vast and hostile, even though today it was blue and tranquil (*pretending to be friendly*, she thought). There had been plenty of times on this adventure when she wished it had never crossed her mind to run away from school with Annalie—when they were escaping from submarine pirates or taking fire from Admiralty marines—but all those other times, the four of them had been together, and their own little boat had been nearby with the promise of escape. Now she was lost, a castaway, in a watery labyrinth; her best friend was far away (if she had even survived), and probably believed she was dead. No help was coming. All hope was lost.

Essie put her head down and burst into tears.

"Oh, don't do that," Will said uncomfortably. "We're going to be okay."

"How can you say that?" Essie sobbed. "We're going to be trapped here forever!"

"No, we're not," Will said. Although his face was contorted with worry, when Essie looked up at him she could see his irrepressible energy already burning through. "I'm going to get us out of here."

"How?" she said.

"I'll think of something," Will said. "We're going to be okay. I promise."

And as unlikely as it seemed, Essie felt she could almost believe him.

Exploring

"The first thing we've got to do is find water. And for that we need plastic."

Will was wrangling plastic from the pile of junk. The first piece he found disintegrated as he tried to extract it—a lot of old plastic was like that—but eventually he found a piece that was still in good shape. He coiled it up carefully and carried it, along with a few other useful things he'd found, down toward the water.

He laid the plastic out flat, measured around it, then set it aside and began to dig until seawater began to seep up into the bottom of the hole. He positioned a container in the middle of his hole, laid the plastic sheeting over the top, and secured it carefully with rocks, shells, and lots of sand to ensure a good seal, placing one final rock on top of the plastic, directly over the container. The seawater seeping up into the hole would be heated by the sun and turn into water vapor; this would condense onto the underside of the plastic surface, and drip down its sloping face into the container as fresh drinking water.

"This is a solar still. It makes fresh water," he explained as he dug.

"Are you sure this works?"

"I know it does. Spinner taught us how to make them. We used to practice living off the land sometimes when we were on holiday."

"Doesn't sound like my kind of holiday," Essie said. "Have you explored the island yet?"

He shook his head.

"Maybe we should," Essie said. "You never know—there could be a shop on the other side."

Will let out a little bark of laughter. They set out to explore.

The island was not much more than a high spine of rock rising out of the ocean, crowned with a healthy covering of trees and shrubs. A narrow strip of sand over rocks lined the cove side; they followed this strip of sand to see where it went. The island rose up steeply above them, foliage wound tightly around the rocky ground, making it seem virtually impenetrable.

"There's plenty of things growing here," Essie remarked. "Do you think that means there's water?"

"Might just mean it gets a lot of rain," Will said.

"I wonder if there are any animals here?"

"There's birds in the trees. Might be having roast seagull for dinner."

"How does seagull taste?"

"Not too good, apparently."

The island ended in a rocky point, which they clambered around. When they emerged from the shelter of the island, they were hit by a strong breeze, which Will quickly realized must be the island's prevailing wind: it had sculpted the trees artistically. Rocks eventually gave way to another thin strip of beach, long, gently curving, and largely uninterrupted. They walked along the beach together, staying on the wet, hard sand. No footprints interrupted its length. No ships showed on the horizon.

"We're going to have to build a proper shelter, aren't we?" Essie sighed.

Will nodded. He felt exhausted just thinking about it. "And find food."

His stomach was so empty it felt like a small animal was trying to eat him from the inside. He turned to look up at the trees rising above them, wondering if there was any chance there might be something edible growing up there—and stopped in his tracks.

"No way," Will said softly.

There, rising above the trees, was a castle.

The castle in the sea

It had what looked like battlements and, above that, a tower.

"What *is* that place?" Essie said, astonished.

"It looks like a castle. Let's go check it out!"

An old, overgrown track led up the hill to the castle, which stood on the highest point of the island, looking out to sea. They stepped out of the trees into an open courtyard where the paving stones were gradually being pushed aside by weeds and tree roots.

Essie stopped to gaze at the large graceful building that rose up before them, its walls covered in carved and painted scenes which had once been vibrantly colorful, before the scouring salt air and wind took all the magic out of them. A mix of stylized human and animal figures interacted mysteriously; they probably told a story, but Essie couldn't guess what it was. "I don't think this is a castle," she said. "I think it's a temple."

"Who cares what it is," Will said. "This place is *awesome!*"

At the entrance was a large pair of carved ornamental doors, once gilded, most of the gold now tarnished and gone. Will gave them a push; they swung open easily. The two of them stepped inside. It took a moment for their eyes to adjust to the light.

"It's so beautiful," Essie said, gazing up at the vaulted ceiling, the tall decorative windows, the ornately patterned floor tiles.

"Hey, look at this!" Will said, his voice filled with excitement.

Someone had been here before them; someone who was entirely of Will's own mind. Carefully sorted and laid out in neat piles was a great quantity of useful stuff. There were containers of different sizes; lengths of rope—alas, none of them very long; plus glass bottles, plastic sheeting, sails, pieces of fishing net, buoys and floats. There were usefully shaped pieces of wood, which looked like they had come from boats, and, beside them, a smaller pile of bits of metal.

Will gazed at it all hungrily. They were exactly the sorts of things he would have collected himself, and he appreciated the thoughtfulness with which they had been arranged. All at once, he was reminded of Spinner's workshop, and homesickness rose in his chest.

"I wonder who collected all this stuff?" he said.

"Someone else must have been stuck here," Essie said.

They looked at each other, hope springing up in their hearts. "Hello?" they called. "Anyone home?"

They called at the tops of their voices, but heard nothing.

"Maybe they've got other stuff too," Will said. "Like a radio transmitter."

"Or a boat!"

They raced off to explore.

They discovered that from the main entrance hall, one door led out to another courtyard—a kind of cloister—green and overgrown. An enclosed walkway surrounded the cloister, with two levels of rooms opening off them. These were all quite empty now, so it was difficult to guess what they'd been used for. Some might have been offices or bedrooms; others might have been classrooms. Behind these were outbuildings that might once have housed a kitchen, laundry, or washing facilities, but had long since been stripped of anything useful.

Another, smaller door opened onto a staircase which led up to the roof. Will and Essie climbed the stairs and stepped out onto the battlements, hoping to spot land or a passing ship, but the sea was empty. They went back into the stairwell and continued to climb. The breeze was murmuring above them and the sunlight filtering down. They emerged into a little tower room.

It had once been a bell tower, and it still stood open to the weather. (The bell had lost its clapper—Will gave it a swing just to test it out, but it was silent.) In spite of the fact it was open to the elements, someone had turned it into a bedroom. A pallet on the floor made a bed, and boxes of different sizes had been stacked against the wall to make storage. A table and a stool—both very simply designed and made, with an old, pre-Flood look—stood under the window that looked out to sea.

Essie looked through the boxes and found a few pieces of grayish clothing; paperback books, a crime thriller and a book of poetry, both with curled, watermarked pages; a toothbrush, very shaggy. Essie thought there was something rather sad about the toothbrush. Meanwhile, Will had found real treasure in the next box: a fishing reel, with plenty of line still attached.

"Look!" he showed her gleefully.

"Yay!" Essie said. "Yummy fish!" She had never particularly liked fish.

Will's pleasure dimmed a little when a search through all the rest of the boxes did not turn up any fishhooks.

"Can you make one?" Essie asked.

"Maybe," Will said, frowning.

There was also nothing resembling food in the tower room.

"I guess he must have taken it with him," Will said. "Whoever he was."

"You think he got off the island?"

"He must have," Will said, not wanting to consider the alternative.

"This really is a pretty amazing place," Essie said. "I wonder who it belongs to?"

"I don't think anyone's lived here for years," Will said. "Decades, probably."

"You think it was abandoned after the Flood?"

"Probably."

Essie looked around her, musing. "So do you think you could just...live here?"

Will looked at her askance. "You mean now? I don't think anyone's going to stop us."

"Well, obviously now," Essie said. "This place is awesome. I guess I just meant...generally."

Will looked around him speculatively. "I don't see why not," he said. "Although you'd always be wondering when the real owners were going to come back. Come on, let's see what else we can find."

They completed their search of the castle with the discovery of the kitchen garden—a few herbs and vegetables survived among the weeds—and the remains of a neat little cooking fire with a little firewood stacked nearby. There were no pots or knives, but they were pleased to discover one fire-blackened frypan.

Will grinned. "Now all we have to do is find something to put in it!"

Delicacies

They continued their circumnavigation of the island, equipped with the hookless fishing reel and some containers Will had found in the great hall of the castle.

Farther down the second beach, the sand ran out and became rocks again. The other end of the island was a fat, rounded teardrop shape, with huge pointed rocks rising to cliffs, tall trees clinging vertiginously to the cliff face, and a lot of prickly undergrowth that snagged at them as they passed. It was hard going climbing round it, but Will did spot a few rock ledges jutting over the ocean with deep holes beside them where he could possibly find fish. Eventually they made their way back to the little cove where they'd started.

"Okay," Will said. "This is where we find some dinner."

He walked along the water's edge for a while, then began to dig. Eventually he let out a cry of triumph and pulled something long and glistening from the sand.

"Gross!" Essie cried. "What is that?"

"Dinner," said Will, with a gleam in his eye.

"You can't be serious," Essie said.

Will, who had responded in exactly the same way when Spinner first showed him a sandworm, gave her a superior look. "They're an excellent source of protein. In some places they're considered a delicacy. Better if you don't chew them, though."

Essie stared at him for a moment more, still hoping he was joking. "Is there *really* nothing else we can eat?" she asked. "Edible seaweed or something?"

"If I can make us a fishhook, they're bait," Will said. "Until then, they're dinner. Are you going to help me dig or what?"

Essie helped dig. They filled their container with sandworms, which writhed about horribly, trying to escape. "Can we at least cook them?" she begged.

"I don't think it'll improve them much," Will said, "but sure."

He built a fire out of driftwood and lit it using an old bottle as a lens.

"It's so cool you know how to do all this stuff," Essie said.

Will enjoyed her admiration, but answered modestly, "Sometimes I wonder whether Spinner was secretly training us to go on the run."

"Just as well he did," Essie said.

Will wrapped the sandworms around a stick and grilled them over the fire, then handed one to Essie and took one himself. Essie squinted at it, screwing up her face.

"On a count of three," Will said. "One—two—three."

They lowered them into their mouths. Essie did her best to swallow hers without tasting it, but didn't quite succeed.

"That's the most disgusting thing I've ever eaten!" she said, when it was down at last.

"They don't taste any better cooked," Will said.

"I thought you said they were a delicacy?"

Will shrugged. "Some people like weird stuff."

"I guess if you're really hungry you'll eat pretty much anything," Essie said.

"Now you're getting it," Will said. "Want another one?"

They ate the rest of them. At first they both felt a bit icky in the stomach, but that passed and some of the raging hunger passed away too, leaving them a little calmer, although not, unfortunately, full.

"So what are we going to do?" Essie asked. She watched Will feeding the fire with sticks. "Should we build a signal fire?"

Will considered. "Sure," he said. "Might as well."

Essie looked at him doubtfully. Something about the way he'd said it made it seem they wouldn't have much need for a signal fire. "You really don't think they're coming back for us?"

"Who, Annalie and Pod? I doubt it."

Essie stared at him now, her anxiety beginning to rise. "They wouldn't just abandon us, would they?"

Will shrugged, poking unhappily at the fire. "You know what the chances are of us surviving a storm like that, and both washing up somewhere safe? They probably think we're already dead."

Essie was silent. She didn't want to believe that Annalie might not be standing by ready to swoop in and rescue them, as she always had before. But then, she hadn't really tried to rescue her when she was washed off the boat, either.

"Annalie saw me, you know," she said softly. "When I went overboard. She tried to throw me the life-preserver but I couldn't get to it." Essie paused. "I thought maybe she'd get the dinghy and try to rescue me, but she didn't. She just turned away and left me to drown." She felt the tears welling up in her eyes and started to cry.

Will looked at her helplessly from across the fire. He hated it when people cried. "Hey, don't do that," he said. "It wasn't like that."

"That's *exactly* what it was like," Essie sobbed.

Will tried awkwardly to explain. "Spinner always taught us that if someone gets washed overboard in a storm, you don't go in after them."

"Why not?" Essie said, shocked.

"Because the most likely thing that'll happen is no one gets rescued and you'll both die," Will said.

"Well, I didn't die," Essie said stubbornly. "Neither did you."

"That's not how it usually pans out, though."

"If it had been you on the boat, what would you have done?" Essie demanded. "Would *you* have gone in after me?"

Will thought about this, and she could see him wrestling with whether or not he should tell her the truth.

"You would, wouldn't you?" she pushed.

"Well, maybe," he admitted. "But it would have been a stupid thing to do." He paused. "I'm kinda known for that."

Essie gave him a half-smile.

"Don't blame Annalie," Will said. "I bet, the way she saw it, if she stayed on the boat and rode out the storm, she could always come and look for us later. If all three of us went overboard, there's no way Pod could have done anything to help. Not all by himself."

Essie could see the logic of this, even though the sense of betrayal still stung. "So you *do* think she's going to come and look for us, then?"

"Well, I hope so," Will said. He could see that Essie didn't find this answer very reassuring—and she needed reassuring. "Don't worry. I'm going to get us off this island. Tomorrow I'll start building a raft."

"We don't have any tools or materials."

"There are loads of materials," Will said. "There's all that stuff up at the castle, and there's plenty more washed up here in the cove. Materials aren't a problem."

"What about tools?"

"Well—yeah," Will admitted. "Tools are a problem. I've still got my pocketknife, but that's it. I'm just going to have to build it out of whatever I can find and lash it all together. I'll need a sail, and something to steer with. We're lucky the prevailing winds ought to take us in the right direction."

"What direction is that?"

"You noticed the wind back on the other beach, right? You can tell by looking at the way the trees all grow that the wind mostly blows from west to east, and that's the way we want to go, toward Dasto Puri."

"How do you know where Dasto Puri is if you don't know where we are?"

"Well, I've got a rough idea. It's somewhere to the east of us. And we need to get there, pronto."

"Why?"

"Because that's where she'll go next. We have to catch up with her before she moves on."

"But she wouldn't move on, would she?" Essie asked, her earlier worries rekindling. "Not without us?"

"I'd rather not have to find out," Will said.

They spent their first night in the castle together in the little tower room.

Essie felt a little shy about sharing a room with Will, but they were both so exhausted they fell asleep almost as soon as they put their heads down.

The castaway life

They woke the next morning, hungry, thirsty, and slightly cold, to the harsh reality of life as castaways. If they wanted food, they had to find it. If they wanted a drink, they had to fetch water. If they wanted a fire, they had to gather the wood, build the fire, and tend it. The warm seas of the archipelago meant the climate was mild, but the nights could be cool, and they had no clothes apart from what they stood up in.

Although Will was eager to get started building his raft, he knew they were going to need more than sandworms to eat. He spent his first morning fashioning a fishhook out of scrap metal.

While he worked, he laid out their plan of attack. "Okay, here's what we're going to do. Today I'm going to teach you how to make a still, how to light a fire and how to fish. That way you can keep us fed and watered while I get the raft built."

"Don't you think we should try and work as a team?" Essie asked.

"We don't have time for that," Will said. "We'll get more done if we split up."

"But we'll work more efficiently if there are two

of us," Essie said.

Will held up the metal he was working. "One fishing reel," he said. "One hook."

"Yes, but once you're building the raft—"

"Someone needs to feed us and someone needs to build," Will said, a little crossly. "Which is it going to be?"

"Fine," Essie said. "I'll fish."

As soon as the fishhook was finished, Will gave Essie crash courses in still-building, fire-lighting, and fishing.

"If you don't know a place, you've got to start by reading the water," he explained as they headed for the rocks at the rounded western end of the island. "Look at the color of the water, where the waves and the still bits are. Where the tide runs. Where there are pools, or drop-offs or rock ledges. You got to look for bait fish too."

"Bait fish?"

"You know those little tiny fish you see swimming around in schools? They're important, because the big fish want to eat them. So where there are bait fish, there are bigger fish, and if you watch the water, and get to know it, you can work out where the big fish might go to catch the little fish."

"You know, you're making this sound very complicated," Essie said. "Don't you just put the hook in and wait for something to bite?"

Will narrowed his eyes at her for a moment, then explained. "Everything in the water is looking for food, and food travels on the tides. Some fish are following the food, others are just waiting until it comes by. Hopefully, we can find a spot where we'll find both." They had reached a long rocky outcrop jutting into the water. "This looks like a good place."

They clambered out to the end of it, and then Will showed her how to bait the hook with some sand-worms they'd dug up along the way. He threw out the line and let it fall into the water. They waited for what seemed to Essie like a long time. Then Will gasped, and began drawing up the line.

It was empty. "Took the bait but not the hook," he said, disappointed. He handed her the reel. "Okay. Your turn."

Essie wincingly jammed the hook through the wriggling worm and dropped it into the water. Again they settled in to wait.

"Do you see how the tide's really moving now?" Will said. "See there? And there? That movement in the water?"

"I guess so," Essie said, although the water didn't really look any different to her. A moment or two later, she thought she felt the line shiver and go taut. "I think I've got something!"

"Here, give it to me!"

Will grabbed the reel from her eagerly and hauled in a fish—not large, but an actual fish. He turned to her with a grin. "There, you see? Easy! Tomorrow, this is your job."

He kept baiting and throwing in the line until he had three fish.

The wait for the right tide, and the fish, had taken most of the afternoon, and they were both hot and thirsty. "Let's go see how your still's doing," Will suggested.

They walked down to the beach where Essie had built her still. It was gone. She stared and stared, and then realized what must have happened. "I think the tide must have washed it away," she said.

Will turned to look at her as if she was a complete idiot. "What? How?"

"I thought it would work better if it had more water coming up into it," Essie explained. "I didn't realize how far the tide was going to come up."

"You can *see* how far the tide comes up!" Will snapped. "You just have to look for the seaweed."

"How was I supposed to know that?" Essie cried.

"It's obvious!" Will said.

"Not to me," Essie said hotly.

They both glared at each other for a moment, then Will turned away from her, shaking his head. "We need to find that plastic."

They spent the next half an hour searching up and down the beach. Eventually Essie spotted it farther down the beach, where it had fetched up among some rocks.

"This stuff is precious," Will said, checking the plastic for damage.

"I know," Essie said.

"Next time you've got to be more careful."

"I know!" Essie snapped.

Will looked at her then, and must have realized he shouldn't push her any further. "Let's build another one," he said.

The next day, Will wanted to start assembling materials for his raft.

"There are some big bits of driftwood down in the cove," he announced. "I'm going to get them out and bring them over to the castle."

Essie thought that sounded like unnecessarily hard work. "Why not just build the boat in the cove?"

"The current's so strong there I'd never be able to launch it," Will said. "And besides, the rest of the materials are already at the castle, so it makes sense to build it there."

When they'd finished their meager breakfast, Will handed her the fishing reel and the bucket. "Your mission," he said, "is to go and get some fish."

"Okay," she said.

And she tried, she really did. She went back to the spot where Will had been successful yesterday. She baited the hook, she threw it in, she waited. There were times when she felt a tug on the line, but when she pulled it up, there was never anything but seaweed, or an empty hook. She baited and threw, baited and threw, again and again, and caught nothing. The morning wore on, hot and sunny. Then she felt something: a tug, a tremble, a shiver on the line. She began to reel it in, afraid of losing it. The tension on the line told her there might be something big on the end. The thought of catching something impressive thrilled her, and she gave a last enthusiastic pull. The line went taut—then suddenly slack.

Essie pulled it up the rest of the way, and what she saw made her heart stop. The line dangled, weightless. The fishhook was gone.

The sun beat down on Will's head. Yet again, he gripped the huge piece of driftwood in both hands and pulled. He had dug it out of the sand now; it should, he thought, be ready to come free. But it was so much heavier than he'd imagined it would be. Huge and silvery, longer than the *Sunfish* and thicker around than his own thigh, he could barely shift it. He struggled and strained; it barely moved; a branch dug into the sand and snagged on a rock. He lost his grip and stopped, puffing. He turned the log, repositioned himself so that he was pushing instead of pulling, and tried again. Agonizingly, he barely got it to move another foot over the sand before his strength gave out and he had to stop.

It had taken him all morning to extract the large, useful bits of driftwood and wreckage from the tangle. He'd laid the pieces out one by one, high on the beach where the sea couldn't take them; the next step would be to transport them all back to the castle. He had thought he would have all the materials there before lunchtime. Now he was beginning to see what a gigantic task he had set himself.

Catching his breath, he blew on his battered, painful hands, and placed them once more on the log, his prize. It was the last one to be pulled free from the tangle. He took a deep breath and heaved.

At first all seemed well—the angle was right, the effort was right, the log was moving—then an unusually big wave swept up and the log rolled, trapping Will's foot beneath it. He fell into the debris, sharp pain stabbing from his foot up into his leg. He pulled, trying to free himself, but his foot was stuck fast, and the log seemed to have become wedged again. Panic surged through him. He tried again to pull his foot free, but it only made the pain worse.

"Essie!" he yelled. "Help!"

No answer came.

The crushing pain in his foot was agonizing, but he tried to think clearly. Maybe if he grabbed the log and rolled it off...

He wrapped his arms around it and tried to move it, but it was hard to get a purchase when he was pinned underneath it. He reached for a big stick and tried to lever up the log, but the stick broke. Another wave washed off the beach and he tried to use the power of the wave to help him shift the log, but it rolled the wrong way and his foot was trapped worse than before.

"Essie!" he called again. "Help!"

But he knew she was too far away to hear him.

Essie returned to the castle, wondering what to do next. The loss of the fishhook was a disaster and she knew Will would blame her for it. *I have to fix this*, she thought. *But how?*

Annalie would know what to do. But Annalie

wasn't here. Essie would just have to come up with something on her own.

She took the stairs up to the tower and gazed out at the sea—brilliant, tranquil, and empty. No boat crossed the horizon. *We could die here*, she thought suddenly.

It might not happen quickly. They might be able to keep themselves alive for days, weeks, months. But something would go wrong, sooner or later. A storm, or an illness. They'd use up all the sandworms. Or they'd lose the fishing reel. And then they'd die, and nobody would ever know what had become of them. Her parents would grow old wondering what had happened to her, and there would be no one left who could tell them.

Tears blurred the sea, but she wiped them away with the back of her hand, struggling to get a grip on herself. Annalie wouldn't collapse into tears like this, and she wasn't going to either. She had to make a new fishhook, or think of something else. Will had talked about roasting seagulls—but how did you catch them? Bird traps? How would you design one? Then another thought came to her: *A slingshot!* She'd never owned such a thing, but she knew what she'd need to make one: a forked stick and something stretchy. Perhaps there might be something down in the piles of old stuff in the great hall?

Inspired, she turned to go downstairs, but caught her toe on the uneven floorboards and went lurching into the stacked up boxes, which tumbled to the floor.

Crossly she began stacking them back up again; as she picked up a box, something stabbed her finger. She jerked her hand back and saw a spot of bright blood well up. She sucked it, looking to see what had stabbed her.

A single fishhook—a *real* fishhook, from a shop, made of bright steel—lay on the floor. She picked it up, gazing at it in astonishment. Why would anyone have left behind such a prize? She realized it must have slipped down between the cracks in one of these boxes, and her lucky accident had jolted it loose.

A wonderful giddy lightness welled up in her. Yes, it was only a fishhook. But it felt like something more: good fortune touching her shoulder, beckoning her on. They were not going to die today.

Triumphantly, she went downstairs to look for the materials to make a slingshot.

Still trapped, Will lay there, the sun beating down on him mercilessly. Nothing he could do would shift the log.

He knew Essie would probably come looking for him eventually, but he had no idea how long that might actually take.

He remembered her asking, *Don't you think we should work as a team?* And how he'd angrily rejected her suggestion. Now it didn't seem like such a bad idea. If they'd been working together, he still might have got stuck, but he wouldn't have spent half the morning trapped under this stupid log. He dreaded to think what might be happening to his foot, which was incredibly painful.

What's going to happen to us if my foot's crushed?

60

he thought, angry with himself. *How can I build a boat and get us off this rock? I won't be able to do anything. And there's no way she can do it without me.*

Guilt and frustration danced through his mind as he tried to imagine teaching Essie to build a raft, launch it, and sail it, while he hopped around with a ruined foot on crutches made of sticks.

It was impossible. They'd never be able to pull it off. Feelings of doom crept over him. *Why didn't I just get her to help me?* he thought bitterly.

He heard a cry, and looked up to see Essie running down the beach toward him.

"Are you okay? What happened? What can I do?" she said breathlessly.

"My foot's trapped and I can't move the log," he said tersely. "But maybe you can."

Essie studied the log, then wrapped both hands around it and lifted. Simple as that, Will rolled free. The weight lifting off his foot sent a fresh surge of pain shooting up his leg.

"Maybe we shouldn't have done that," Essie said worriedly. "Crush injuries can be really bad."

"No, it's okay," Will said through clenched teeth. The pain really was excruciating. "Better than being trapped under that log."

"In *Below Decks: Courage*, one of the lieutenants got crushed by a door in a sea battle, and they knew that as soon as they took him out of the door he'd die because of the crush injuries, so he had to say good-bye to everybody first," said Essie.

"What?"

"Sorry. *Below Decks*. It was one of my favorite vid shows, that's all. But forget about that, you're not going to die. Should we get you back to the castle?"

Will nodded. He slung an arm across her shoulders and together they hopped slowly and painfully up the path.

"Do you want to go up to the tower?" Essie suggested, rather dreading the thought of all those stairs, but Will sank down on the floor of the great hall beside the front door.

"Here is fine," he said.

The two of them studied Will's foot. It had darkened like a storm cloud and looked puffy and swollen.

"Do you think anything's broken?" Essie asked. "Try and wiggle your toes."

Will did, and hissed with pain. "It hurts," he said, "but I don't *think* anything's broken."

"Why don't I go and get you some water?" Essie said. "You need to rest. And you should probably elevate that foot to help the swelling go down."

She found something for him to put his foot on, then left to get water. She was gone a long time. Will was starting to get impatient when at last the main doors swung open again.

"Ta da!" she cried.

Essie stood there in the doorway, holding a jar of water in one hand, and in the other, a bucket of fish.

"Hey, you caught some!" Will said.

"Don't sound so surprised," Essie said. "And look what else I've got."

She showed him the reel with its real, shiny fishhook dangling from the end. Will's eyes went round with wonder. "Where did—"

"And that's not all," Essie said. She fetched the slingshot from her back pocket and held it out to him. "I tried to bring down a seagull, but I haven't really got the hang of it yet."

Will took it from her and examined it, a slow smile spreading across his face. He looked up at Essie with a grin. "Who knew you were such a bad-ass?" he said.

They sat down to eat lunch that had been caught, scaled and gutted—so many new and disgusting skills!—entirely by Essie.

"You know," Will said, once they'd eaten, "maybe it *would* be more efficient if we worked as a team."

Essie looked over at him and smiled a little. She could have gloated. But all she said was, "Sure."

Will's foot did not turn out to be broken, although it did turn all the colors of the rainbow over the next few days. Soon enough he was hobbling about again, giving Essie pointers on her fishing technique, refining the design of their solar still, and practising with Essie's slingshot until he could reliably knock a seagull out of a tree. They kept a lookout for boats on the horizon, but saw nothing. For the first few days, Essie worried that, because they were working so hard, they might not have noticed the boats as they passed. But gradually they came to realize that the reason they hadn't seen any boats was because there weren't any.

"Where are they all?" Essie said. "We're still in the Moon Islands. Isn't it supposed to be full of pirates and refugees?"

"Well, yes... and no."

"What does that mean?"

"It means there are a lot of places to hide here. And to get lost in."

"This place would make a brilliant hide-out," Essie said. "Think about what you could do with it if you could fix it up a bit."

"It'd be awesome," Will said.

"Wouldn't it?" Essie said. "I mean, if you had some power and some proper food and stuff. You could live here and it'd be amazing."

"You'd never have to worry about the Admiralty tracking you down," said Will.

"Maybe, if we ever get out of this, we can come back here one day and fix it up for ourselves," Essie said dreamily.

"You mean to live?" Will asked. "For real?"

"Why not?" Essie said. "I mean, maybe not *all* the time. But it'd be cool to have it as a secret base, wouldn't it?"

"Totally cool," Will said, the idea growing on him. They were both silent for a moment, mentally decorating.

"Now all we have to do is get out of here and find the others," Essie said.

Good-bye castle

It took them several weeks to get the raft ready. It was made out of driftwood and the largest pieces of buoyant rubbish from the inlet. There was a central platform where the two of them would ride along with their supplies, and pontoons on either side for stability. Will had put up a mast and made a small square-rigged sail out of the blue tarp. There was a rudder, and some oars in case they needed to row.

"Okay," Will said. "Let's test this thing and see if it floats."

The raft, perhaps unsurprisingly, was enormously heavy. Even with the two of them pushing and heaving with all their might, they could hardly move it down the beach. After they had pushed it a foot or two—and still had many more to go before they reached the water—Will stepped away, panting.

"You know," he said, "even if we do manage to get it down to the water, I don't think we're going to be able to get it out again."

Essie still had spots dancing in front of her eyes from the effort. "No," she agreed. "So what do we do?"

65

"I think," Will said, "we'd better pack it up here on the shore, wait until the tide's high, and then launch it."

"Without a trial run?"

"Yep."

Essie paused for a moment, thinking about all the objections she should be raising: *We don't know where we're going. We have no way to navigate. What about storms? What about sharks? What if it takes weeks and we run out of food and water? What if where we're going is worse than where we are now, where at least we have shelter and can feed ourselves?*

But all she said was, "Okay."

They packed their supplies as carefully as they could, a task complicated by the fact they didn't have proper containers for anything, or much in the way of rope. Will kept one eye on the tide as they loaded their stores. It washed gently up the beach, higher and higher, until at last it was time to go.

"Okay," he said. "Let's give this another try."

They leaned their shoulders into the raft and pushed and struggled and pushed and heaved. The waves began to lick the pontoons. Essie and Will strained and struggled and pushed some more. The front of the raft reached the water's edge, and they felt it being lifted and moved by the tide.

"Push when the waves are going out!" Will directed, and they used the motion of the waves to move the raft until at last it floated free. Will clambered aboard, pulling Essie up after him, and took one of the long oars to push off against the shallow bottom.

"She floats!" Essie said joyfully.

"Let's hope she hangs together," Will said.

Essie watched the sandy bottom drop away beneath them. The water changed from blue to a deep green and soon the bottom was no longer visible at all. The little sail flapped and caught the wind.

"How good is this!" he cried. "Didn't I tell you I'd get us off the island?"

"I never doubted it," Essie said. She turned to look at him, and saw how unambiguously happy he was to be on the water again—happiness radiated from him.

"You really love all this, don't you?" she said.

"It's the best thing in the world," he said, and grinned.

The island, topped by its crenellated tower, began slowly to recede.

"Good-bye, castle," Essie said, watching it go. Will's high spirits were infectious, and it felt good to be on their way once more. Unknown dangers lay ahead of them. But if all went well, and their luck held, soon, perhaps, they would be reunited with Annalie, Pod, Graham, and the *Sunfish*.

The Loudon Multi-Phasal Scanning Module

"Let me get this straight," Wirehead said. "You want us to fix your boat, look for your missing friends, and help you track down this Dan Gari?"

"Correct," Annalie said.

She was sitting with Pod in Wirehead's office, a handsomely decorated room with a tall executive chair behind a huge desk and a lot of high-end devices on custom-made shelves. After arriving on the island, they had been given a place to stay and then left alone for a day, presumably while Wirehead went away and checked out their story. Now they had been summoned to his office.

"So, how were you planning to pay for all that?" Wirehead asked.

"I was hoping you or your friends might know how to get in touch with Spinner," Annalie said.

"Nope," Wirehead said, smiling blandly. "What else have you got?"

Annalie did have some money, mostly supplied by Essie. They usually kept it hidden aboard the *Sunfish,* but she and Pod had divided it up and hidden it inside their clothing before coming ashore. She knew that the money would not be enough, so it was best to keep it to herself.

"Could we trade you something from the boat to pay for the repairs?" Annalie asked.

Wirehead raised an eyebrow, reaching for a list. He scanned it, then looked back at her. "Nothing you have on your boat is worth anywhere near enough," he said coolly.

Annalie realized the list must be an inventory of the *Sunfish*'s contents. She was relieved they hadn't left the money behind for the pirates to find. "Is there some other way we can pay?" she asked.

From the corner of her eye she saw Pod scowl at her, but she knew she had no other option.

"As a matter of fact," Wirehead said, "there is."

Wirehead picked up a shell and activated the display. An image of a piece of computer hardware was projected into the air between them.

"This is the Loudon Multi-Phasal Scanning Module," Wirehead said. "It's part of the Admiralty's new-generation weather array, and it's much better than anything they've had before. They're rolling it out to their top-of-the-line vessels at the moment, and we want one." Wirehead rotated the image, which turned in 3D, revealing its various angles. "I want you to steal it for me."

"I don't know anything about thieving," Annalie protested. "Why do you need me to do it?"

"We need someone small," Wirehead said. "Like you."

The Admiralty had a base on the eastern edge of

the Moon Islands. There was a technical crew there that did the high-end maintenance that couldn't be done at sea, including upgrading and installing the newest technology. The Kangs had discovered the base had recently received one of these modules; their spies had identified which warehouse it was kept in, and acquired the code that would let you into the storeroom where it was kept. They had also identified a tiny window, high up on the perimeter wall, which a small thief could wriggle through.

"So what do you think?" Wirehead said. "Are you game?"

"If I can get this device for you," Annalie said, checking the terms of the deal, "you'll fix my boat?"

"Yes."

"And you'll help me find my friends? And Dan Gari?"

"Yes, yes."

Pod jumped in. "We'll be totally square? No bills, no extra money owing?"

Wirehead smiled. "Didn't I tell you I'm an honest gentleman of the sea?"

"And once the boat's fixed, we'll be able to leave here on it, free and clear?" Annalie said.

"That is the nature of the deal, yes," Wirehead said, starting to sound irritated. "So what's it going to be? Yes or no?"

Pod looked at Annalie. "Are you sure about this?" he murmured.

"What choice do we have?" Annalie said.

"None," Wirehead said. "Let's go steal some tech!"

The *Sunfish* would have taken weeks to get to the Admiralty base, but the Kangs didn't move at such a leisurely pace. That same day, Annalie and Pod were loaded into the back of a Kang boat, and soon they were motoring through the rocky channels of Dasto Puri and out into the open sea. Annalie had told Graham to stay with the *Sunfish* while they were gone, but Graham didn't trust the pirates. "Graham go ashore. Graham like land. Find nice tree."

"Please be careful," Annalie said.

"You be careful," Graham retorted.

Annalie had also tried to tell Pod that he didn't have to come with her on the mission, but Pod was having none of it.

"It's my boat," she said. "I made the deal. No point both of us going down for it."

"Who's going to keep you out of trouble if I don't come?" Pod said.

Wirehead insisted they spend some time studying the device as they traveled. The storeroom would be full of tech; any of it, obviously, would be welcomed by the Kangs, but he wanted to be absolutely sure they stole the right device.

Not far from the island where the Admiralty base was located, they met with a rickety-looking fishing boat that would take them ashore. The Kangs were not so foolish as to take one of their own vessels into the Admiralty's harbor. Annalie, Pod

71

and Wirehead clambered across from the Kang boat onto the fishing boat, which reeked, unsurprisingly, of fish. The Kang boat roared off to wait at a safe distance while the fishing boat puttered toward their destination.

"Just remember," Wirehead warned them as they entered the harbor, "if you try to go to the Admiralty about your mission, you're dead. Tell them what we're looking for, tell them we put you up to it, try to make trouble for us, you're dead. Understand? If I hear you've snitched—and I *will* hear—you're dead. Doesn't matter what deals you think you've made with them, you're dead. We got eyes everywhere. We know everything. So don't even try it. Okay?"

Annalie gulped and nodded. She had no doubt that he meant it.

The Admiralty base was vast and sprawling, made up of a huge assortment of buildings both old and new, ringed around with walls and fences. They walked and walked, through the civilian town that surrounded the base, along busy streets filled with bustling night markets, past places to eat and drink and be entertained, and then on to the warehouse district. There, most of the buildings had already been locked up, and the few people who remained were in a hurry to get home. There were no streetlights here, and although one or two warehouses had their own light over the door, they did little to penetrate the gloom.

Finally Wirehead stopped in a street filled with rundown warehouses and nodded toward a building. "There it is."

The building was made of dark old brick, two storeys high, with just a few small windows in the otherwise blank facade. There were no KEEP OUT signs, no warnings. No lights shone from anywhere inside. It was so dark they could barely even see the window they were supposed to climb through.

"Go on," Wirehead said. "Don't muck this up."

Thieves

The window was indeed tiny. Annalie squeezed through, and Pod followed. He was rake-thin, but his shoulders were broader than hers, and for a moment it looked like he was stuck, but somehow he managed to squirm through.

The warehouse was entirely dark. Wirehead had told them that at night the building was locked up and there were guards on all the doors, but they were stationed outside; they shouldn't expect to see anyone inside. Following their hand-drawn map, the two of them hurried down the hallway. Every step seemed to echo; although Annalie knew no one was supposed to be in the building, every sound grated on her nerves. She tried to tread more quietly.

They found the storeroom without difficulty. Annalie hesitated over the numeric keypad, stopping yet again to check the number she had memorized. She entered it, afraid that this might be the moment it all went wrong, fearing a light would turn red and an alarm start wailing.

The door gave a cheery chirp and a click. They pushed the door open and stepped into a large warehouse filled with metal shelving which ran floor to ceiling. It reminded Annalie of Spinner's workshop at home, although everything Spinner had was second-hand, home-made, reconditioned. Everything here was fresh from the factory, brand new and shiny. It was shelved according to numbers and codes, which would have made it easy to find what you were looking for if you knew the code. Unfortunately, the Kangs had not provided them with that information.

"Let's split up," Pod whispered. "Be quicker."

Annalie started at one end of the warehouse, Pod at the other, and the two of them began working their way down the aisles. Annalie shone her flashlight on rows and rows of gadgets, realising it could take them hours to find what they were looking for.

"Hey, Annalie," hissed Pod. "Come look at this."

She hurried to join him at the far end of the store-room. To her dismay, she saw him shining his light on a secure area of shelving protected by a metal cage.

"Reckon that's where they keep the good stuff?" Pod said.

Annalie shone her flashlight through the bars and ran it along shelves filled with expensive-looking high-tech gear. Sure enough, there, in the middle of a row, was the Loudon Multi-Phasal Scanning Module.

"How are we going to get in there?" Annalie said, dismayed.

Pod walked over to the gate. It had a keypad, just like the main door. "Reckon it's the same number?" he suggested.

"Wouldn't be very secure if it was," Annalie said, inspecting the keypad. "Why didn't the Kangs find out *this* number? We can't do anything without it."

"Maybe there's some other way to get in," Pod said.

They prowled around the cage, studying it. The bars were too close together for even a skinny child to slip through, and went right down to the floor, so there was no chance of sneaking underneath. There was a metal roof sitting squarely on top of the bars, so there was no way of sneaking over the top either. They returned their attention to the gate.

"Maybe it has another key?" Annalie said. There was a desk beside the cage, where a guard presumably sat during the day. She began to examine the desk. "Maybe there's some kind of manual release. A spare key, or a button you can press."

"If you find one, don't press it," Pod said. "It's probably alarmed."

Annalie took half a step back, afraid of accidentally triggering anything. "I don't know what to do," she said helplessly.

Pod had returned to study the gadget through the bars thoughtfully. "You reckon it's small enough to fit through the bars?" he asked.

Annalie came and joined him. "The box is too big," she said.

"Yeah, but what about the thing itself?"

Annalie raised her eyebrows. There was probably padding inside the box to protect the gadget, which meant the device itself might just be small enough to get through the bars. "Maybe."

"Okay, then."

Pod moved away purposefully, hunting the aisles. When he came back, he held a coil of thin, lightweight cable. He took out his pocketknife, attached it to the cable, then chose a blade with a hook on the end. Carefully he leaned through the bars and swung the cable toward the gadget on the shelf. His first throw missed. He tried again; this time he clipped the box, but the hook didn't take. He tried this several more times, but it soon became clear it wasn't going to work. The hook simply couldn't grab onto the box.

"I've got another idea," Annalie said.

She went back to the security desk, opened a few drawers, and soon found what she was looking for: a roll of tape. She made a sticky loop of tape, and stuck it as securely as she could onto the hook.

"Try it now," she said.

Pod swung the cable again. The tape stuck. "Got it!" Pod whispered in triumph.

Carefully Pod eased the box off the shelf and dragged it to the bars. Annalie reached in and unpacked it, removing the components from their packaging one by one and easing them through the bars as delicately as if she was moving a baby bird that had fallen from its nest. Pod amused himself hooking some other objects from inside the cage and adding them to their haul.

"That's not what we came for, you know," she reminded him.

"Who cares? It's good tech," Pod said. "Pirates always want good tech. Maybe we can earn ourselves a bonus."

Annalie grinned and jammed everything into a backpack. "Okay," she said, "let's get out of here."

The two of them hurried for the door, but before they could reach it, they heard a sound that stopped them cold.

There were voices coming from somewhere outside. Suddenly, light bloomed under the door.

There were people in the corridor. And they were coming in.

Lost on the base

Pod and Annalie scampered back to hide in one of the rows, crouching behind some huge drums.

"Is there another way out?" Pod whispered.

"I don't think so," she said.

"Windows?" Pod said.

They swivelled to look, and yes, there were windows, high up in the walls.

"We could climb up the shelves," Pod said.

They ran to the end of the row and the window furthest from the door. Pod climbed up first, his long limbs making short work of the climb. The shelves wobbled dangerously under him—they were freestanding and were not intended for this kind of treatment. Annalie climbed cautiously after Pod, afraid of toppling the whole thing over and starting a chain reaction that would bring all the rows of shelves down like dominoes. Pod, up on top, extended a hand to help her up.

Outside the door, they heard beeping. Someone was keying in the code.

Pod pushed at the window. "It doesn't open," he said. "We're going to have to break it."

The door chirped and opened. Someone slapped on the lights. The sudden brightness was dazzling.

Pod put his foot against the glass and kicked hard; Annalie joined in. The window shattered and they knocked the pieces of glass out.

Someone shouted, and they could hear booted feet running. Pod wrapped his hand in a fold of his shirt, lowered himself out the window, and dropped.

Annalie did her best to follow, but as she gripped the window ledge, glass stabbed deep into her hand, and the sudden bright pain made her lose her grip and she fell, landing awkwardly so one foot crumpled under her. More pain blazed up her leg. Pod helped pull her to her feet.

They had landed in a courtyard, and Annalie realized to her dismay they were now inside the Admiralty base. There was just enough light to see two fugitive kids, if you were looking for them.

"This way," Pod said, and pulled her into the darkness between two buildings. Annalie hopped along after him, fiery pain shooting up and down her leg. *This is bad*, she thought. *This is really bad*.

They dropped down out of sight, both of them gasping.

"What are we gonna do now?" Pod said.

"We've got to find a way to get off this base."

"That map any use?"

"Nope." It only had the floorplan for the warehouse, nothing more.

"Which way do you reckon?"

"Your guess is as good as mine," Annalie said.

Her hand was throbbing. She peered at it in the darkness and realized blood was welling out of it. "My hand's bleeding."

"We don't want to leave a trail," Pod said.

He took out his pocketknife again, sliced a strip off the bottom of his shirt, and used it to bandage the cut. It did nothing to stop the throbbing pain, but she hoped it would stem the bloodflow.

"They must know we're out here," Pod said. "We should keep moving. They're gonna come looking for us."

With no idea which direction they should be going in, they hurried away. Annalie's leg hurt so much she could barely hobble. Pod kept getting ahead of her and having to wait for her to catch up. Eventually he said, "Here," and offered her his arm. Together they limped along, trying to stay in the shadows. The sounds of feet and voices seemed to be everywhere, echoing nightmarishly off the hard surfaces around them. They walked up this row of buildings and down that, choosing the darkest streets, ducking down to hide whenever anybody came near them. In no time at all they were hopelessly lost, with absolutely no idea how they were ever going to get off the base.

Once, they came out from a gap between two buildings and actually spotted a gate. It was brilliantly lit and heavily guarded. No one could pass in or out without having their identity checked and their purpose noted.

"We could make a run for it," said Pod.

"They've got motorbikes," Annalie said. "And I don't think I can run."

81

"Steal a motorbike?"

"Seriously?"

"Find a truck and hide in it?"

"I bet they'd search them."

Someone was coming toward them. Once again they were forced to retreat.

"Maybe we'll find another gate," Annalie said.

They kept moving, rather hopelessly now. Annalie was having to lean more and more heavily on Pod. And she was beginning to worry that Wirehead would give them up for lost and leave without them.

Then a smell caught her attention, a smell she remembered from school: the throat-catchingly fierce scent of Admiralty laundry. "Maybe we can make ourselves a bit less conspicuous," she said.

They were standing outside the laundry building, and luckily it wasn't locked. Inside, a collection room held bags of clean laundry, each bag neatly labeled with its owner's name, rank and number. She searched the rows until she found what she was looking for.

"Here you go, Cadet Pod. Try this on for size."

Pod's jumpsuit was too short, and Annalie's too long, but they made passable cadets, so long as you didn't look at their feet: Pod wore no shoes at all, and Annalie wore old canvas sandshoes. Real cadets would have worn boots, but they couldn't be too fussy. Annalie picked up one of the laundry bags and concealed her backpack inside it.

"We can't keep wandering around trying to find a gate we can get through," she said. "They'll all be like that first one—too many guards. I think we need to try and get back to that warehouse and leave the way we came."

"Seriously?" Pod said.

"Yes. They'll search the place, and when they realize we're not there any more, they'll leave again. They won't be expecting us to come back."

"So how do we find that warehouse again?"

"I think I can work it out."

Annalie's old boarding school, Triumph College, was attached to an Admiralty battleship. She'd been on the battleship's base several times during her only term at Triumph and she knew there was an order to the way they were laid out. The Admiralty liked grids, and they liked numbers. She consulted her map once more and saw, to her great relief, that whoever had drawn the map had also written the building's number on it. The warehouse they'd broken into was building J207.

"I reckon," Annalie said, "the letter tells you what street it's on, and then you just have to follow the numbers."

"So where are we now?"

Annalie took Pod outside, and they saw the laundry building was numbered C466.

"That sounds far."

"Maybe. Maybe not. Let's go."

They hobbled on, two dodgy-looking cadets carrying a laundry sack. Annalie's guess proved correct, and they soon found their way to J street. The buildings on J seemed to be mostly storage rooms and workshops rather than messes or dormitories, and at night most of these were dark, quiet and empty. But even this part of the base was not deserted; guards passed them more than once, actively patrolling.

"I don't think they've given up yet," Pod whispered. There had been something intent and focused about the way the guards shone their torches into every nook and cranny.

At last they reached J207. They peered out of a dark doorway to see if there was anyone watching the door.

"There's no one on guard," Annalie said.

"That's stupid," Pod said. "*I* would have put a guard on if it was *my* tech."

Annalie didn't care whether it was stupid or not. Escape seemed very close now, and she wasn't about to start questioning it. "Maybe this is our lucky day. Let's just figure out how we get back in."

Pod already had a plan. "I go back in the same window. You give me a boost. Then I pull you up."

Annalie was tired, her hand was throbbing badly, and her leg was killing her. It sounded good enough to her. "Okay," she said. "Let's do it."

The two of them stepped out of the doorway and began to hurry toward the warehouse.

A voice rang out. "Hey, you! Cadets! Stop there!"

Cadet Annalie

Pod and Annalie froze and turned around.

A tiny red glowing light brightened and dimmed, then an officer stepped out of the darkness. He'd been sneaking a quiet cigarette, something you weren't supposed to do on base. In the darkness, they hadn't noticed him.

"It's well after 22:00. Why aren't you in barracks?"

Pod was rooted to the spot, but Annalie kept her head. She snapped to attention. Pod did his best to follow suit.

"Sorry, sir," she said. "It's my fault, sir. Forgot to pick up my laundry today. It's got my parade kit in it, and if I'm not in perfect order for parade tomorrow, my whole bunk's going to suffer for it. And then they'll make *me* suffer."

The officer narrowed his eyes at Annalie, then turned his attention to Pod. "That doesn't explain what *you're* doing out of barracks."

Pod could see he would have to say something. He had no idea what might or might not make a convincing lie. "I was hungry," he said.

The officer was silent again, considering. "You

certainly look like you need feeding up," he said finally. "What barracks are you in?"

"Gold, sir," Annalie said crisply.

The officer's brows drew together into a slight frown. Was that doubt in his eyes? Had she said the wrong thing? For a long, horrible moment it seemed that they were about to be exposed as impostors. Finally the officer spoke. "Well, hurry up then," he said. "Get back to barracks. And next time, try and be more organized."

"Yes, sir, thank you, sir. I will, sir."

Annalie and Pod took off, hurrying away from the warehouse once more. It took all of Annalie's willpower to walk without hobbling. They couldn't afford to make the officer suspicious.

As soon as they were out of sight, they sank down and hid. The pain in Annalie's leg was hideous, and she wasn't entirely sure she'd be able to get up again. They lay there, exhausted, both their hearts racing, waiting to see what would happen next. Not long afterward, the officer strolled past, his hands in his pockets, whistling tunelessly.

Once he was gone, Annalie spoke. "Let's get out of here before someone tells him he should be looking for intruders."

They went back to the warehouse. This time there was nobody about. Annalie braced herself against the wall, laced her fingers together, and boosted Pod up the wall. The pressure of his foot made her hand start bleeding again, and when he climbed up on her shoulders to reach for the window she thought she'd collapse under his weight. It was very high, but Pod was both strong and determined. He slung the laundry bag up onto the window to protect them both from the remaining glass, then hauled himself up. Once inside, he dangled a spare jumpsuit out the window for Annalie, and somehow managed to pull her up the wall and into the room.

It was just as dark as they had left it, and they hurried to the door. It was locked; this gave them a few anxious moments until Annalie discovered the door release and set them free. Then it was only a few moments more until they were through the last window and dropping into the street outside.

Wirehead sauntered up. "What took you so long?"

The Weather Man

It was going to take some time to repair the *Sunfish*, so Annalie, Pod, and Graham had no choice but to wait. The pirates had given them a tiny lean-to to sleep in during their stay. It was tacked onto the back of a kitchen and smelled of old cooking fat, with just one small window and a floor of cracked concrete. Two thin, stained pieces of foam rubber were the only bedding, and the room had no other furniture. The pirates themselves had nicer quarters, but as Pod explained, the nicer their quarters were, the more they'd have to pay for them.

Nothing came for free on Dasto Puri. The room they'd been given, the medical treatment Annalie received for her cut hand and sprained ankle, the food they ate in the communal mess hall, even the biscuits they got for Graham—all of it was being added to their bill. "The less we eat," Pod warned, "the less we'll owe." But the Kangs, it turned out, kept a rather good communal table, and they couldn't help eating enthusiastically almost every time they went in there.

Annalie did her best to hold Wirehead to the deal they'd made. The way she saw it, he'd promised to fix the boat, find Dan Gari, and help them search for

Will and Essie. The first two things could wait, but the search for the others could not.

"I'll put the word out about your friends," Wirehead said, not with any great enthusiasm. "If they're out there, someone will find them."

"But can't you organize a search party? Send someone out? We'd be happy to go ourselves if you'd just lend us a boat."

"Lend you a boat? Do you know what my people have to do to earn a boat?" he said, offended. "We don't *lend* our boats to anyone."

"I'm sorry," Annalie said, "I just really need to find them."

"I said I'll put the word out," Wirehead said. "That's the best I can do." He paused. "So, did you still want to see Dan Gari?"

A Kang guard escorted them up the narrow path that led up from the town and switchbacked up the cliff to the top of the island. This path, they would later discover, continued on around the island's high circumference and led to the lookout posts and defensive emplacements dotted around the cliffs, protecting every approach. Looming above it all, on the highest part of the island, was a tower, sturdily constructed in a military sort of way. The top of the tower was all windows, like the top of a lighthouse, ringed by a metal catwalk. The windows were reflective, so it was impossible to see inside, but the roof above it bristled with instrumentation of every kind.

"What do you suppose that is?" Pod asked.

Their Kang escort spoke up. "That's the Weather Man's crib. Most of us have never even been inside it."

They reached the foot of the tower. The Kang pressed a buzzer; a camera swivelled; they were examined; the door beeped and the Kang opened it.

"The Weather Man's waiting," he said.

Annalie and Pod stepped inside; the Kang didn't follow. He took up a position outside the door, standing guard, and let the door swing shut again.

"Enough security?" Annalie whispered.

"Pirates," Pod replied, also in a whisper. "Paranoid."

They were at the base of a circular staircase. There was nowhere to go but up, so they went up. Doors opened off the staircase as they climbed; all were closed and secured with electronic locks. When they reached the top of the staircase, they were confronted with yet another door. Annalie pressed the buzzer. Another camera focused on them, there was a definite pause, and then this door, too, opened.

They stepped into a room as wide as the tower itself. It was entirely walled with windows, but the glass had been darkened to reduce the glare, so the room had a twilight look. In the center of the room was a huge console stacked to the ceiling with screens and readouts, instruments and displays. The amount of information on display was dizzying, all of it updating and changing and refreshing every moment. It seemed hard to believe any one person could keep track of this much data, and yet the console only had a single chair in front of it. All these readouts were the responsibility of one man.

That man was standing awkwardly behind his chair, looking as if he rarely had visitors and didn't know what to do with himself. He was pale, with a round belly and a bald head. He had none of the swagger of most Kangs, who liked to dress up in fancy waistcoats and jaunty hats and purple kerchiefs. This man wore baggy green shorts, plastic sandals, and a huge shapeless T-shirt with the name of a pre-Flood vid about a space war on it. The look on his face was too blank to be hostile, but it was not exactly welcoming either.

"I heard you've been looking for me," he said.

"Are you Dan Gari?"

He nodded.

Annalie wouldn't have recognized him from the photograph Essie had found, but then this man had the kind of indistinct face you'd forget within five minutes of meeting him. "My name's Annalie Wallace. I'm Spinner's daughter."

She'd hoped he might smile or look a bit more friendly at the mention of Spinner's name. Instead, he frowned. "Is that supposed to mean something to me?"

"You must remember Spinner. Ned Wallace? You worked together, a long time ago."

"You want something from me," Gari said. "What is it?"

Anxiety was beginning to seep into Annalie's mind, making it hard to think clearly. "Help," she said. "Information."

"About the weather?"

"About *Spinner*," Annalie said, starting to become frustrated. "Has he been in contact with you? Has he been here?"

"I don't think I have anything to say to you on that subject," Gari said.

"But he left me your name and address. You were on a list."

"A list?" Gari said, looking alarmed. "What list?"

"I think you know what list," Annalie said.

Gari reached for his console and pressed a button. "Hey, you, whatever your name is, can you come up here, please? You shouldn't have let these people in."

Annalie realized she and Pod were about to get thrown out—or worse. "No wait, please—"

"You could be Admiralty spies for all I know," Dan Gari said.

"I'm not a spy!" Annalie cried. "I'm Annalie Wallace!"

Pod spoke for the first time. "She can prove it."

"How?" Gari said suspiciously.

"We've got Graham. Spinner's parrot. You must remember him."

Gari frowned, then said, "Show me."

The guard took Pod back down to the town. Pod soon returned with Graham on his shoulder.

"Graham," Pod said. "Do you remember this man?"

Graham fluttered to the back of Gari's chair and peered into the man's face. "Danny Boy?" he inquired after a moment.

Gari's eyebrows went up slowly.

"Hair gone," Graham said. "You got fat."

"Manners, Graham!" Annalie said.

Graham *skrarked*. "Too old for manners."

There was a moment of silence. Then Gari said, "I always wondered how Spinner put up with you."

"Graham charming boy," Graham said, and fluffed himself up.

Gari turned to Annalie. "You look more like her than him," he said in an abrupt sort of way.

"So you do remember Spinner?"

"Course I do," Gari said. "But I'm not going to talk about him to just anyone. I had to be sure."

"You couldn't tell just by looking at me?"

"They could've found someone who looked right. Coached you about what to say."

"Who could?"

"The Admiralty, of course. So, this list...does it really exist?"

Annalie nodded. "Spinner left it for me—it was in code. You're on it, and so are Sola Prentice, Ganaman Kiveshalan and Sujana Kieferdottar."

"He didn't tell me he'd done that," Gari said fretfully.

"You've spoken to him?" Annalie asked eagerly.

"Oh yes," Gari said. "He was here."

"Really? When?"

"A few weeks ago."

"Is he still here?" Annalie asked.

"No. He couldn't stay here."

"Why not?"

"With the Admiralty on his tail? They wouldn't tolerate it." By "they" he clearly meant the Kang Brotherhood. Annalie thought it was interesting he didn't say *we*. "Anyway, he didn't want to stay. He's going to see all the others."

Annalie looked at Pod with pleasure and relief. "So we *are* on the right track," she said. Back on Little Lang Lang, Uncle Art had suggested that the voyage to the Moon Islands had just been a ruse and that Spinner might never have actually left Dux. Now they knew for certain he really was here—somewhere. "So he was coming to see you?" she asked. "What did he come here for?"

"To figure out what to do, of course."

"You mean, what to do with the stolen research?"

Gari looked at her suspiciously. "It was our research. I'm not sure it's stealing if you created it in the first place." He caught himself. "What do you know about that?"

"We know you were researching the Collodius Process, but you began to worry the work was going to be used for the wrong reasons."

"We had no doubt they were going to use it for the wrong reasons," Gari said. "There was no other reason for doing the research they had us doing. They wanted to build the device again."

"But why?" Annalie asked.

"They didn't tell us why. Maybe they were hoping to work out a way to reverse it, maybe they wanted to engineer another flood event. We didn't know; they wouldn't tell us. That information was even more top secret than the work we were doing."

"Surely they must have told you something," Annalie said.

"You don't know much about military organizations, do you, little lady?" Gari said patronizingly. "They tell you what they think you need to know and no more. So we were in the dark about their motives. All we had to go on was the direction of the work. And they were definitely pushing us toward the rebuild stage."

"Is that what you stole?" Annalie asked. "Plans to rebuild the device?"

"The *device* is the least of it," Gari said, sounding increasingly grand as he warmed to the story. "The device is just a gadget. The hardware, that was Spinner's part. But the device is nothing without all the other elements: the precise chemical formula to change the way water disperses. The correct atmospheric level for deployment. The weather modeling that tells you where it's going to go. Not to mention all the other modeling that tracked every other variable: the heat in the atmosphere, the effect of increased weather volatility on rainfall, where the water used to be, where it is now, how it behaves under these new conditions, what's been going on in the forty years since the last event."

"What *has* been going on?" Annalie asked.

"You have to understand, the Collodius Process didn't just cause a flood. It changed *everything*. It changed *rain*. It changed *clouds*. We're still trying to work out how all of it fits together now—the wind, the currents, everything that *makes* weather. And you can't do that without data. Reams of data. Mountains of data. And we don't have that data, because not even the Admiralty can keep track of the whole world."

"It looks like *you're* collecting a lot of data," Annalie observed.

"I am," he said, glancing with pride and affection at his readouts. "The Kangs think all this is for them." He smirked, then realized what he'd said. "A lot of it *is* for them, of course. I make sure they've got better information about weather and the oceans than the Admiralty. Trust me, the Admiralty's got no one who's better at this than me. And thanks to my Kang brothers, I've got all the best tech too. But forecasting the weather for pirates doesn't require an array like this."

"What *is* it for?" Annalie asked.

"The work, of course," Gari said. "The Collodius Process. I'm still tracking it. Still tracing the effects. It's still flowing through the system, and we have to study it. It's the only way we'll ever really know what they did to our world."

"But who are you doing the research for?" Annalie asked.

"For? What do you mean?"

"You're not doing it for the Kangs. And I presume you don't want to share it with the Admiralty."

"And get thrown in prison for the rest of my life? And that's the best-case scenario. Not a chance."

"Then who is it for?"

Gari paused, his grandiose tone faltering. "For my colleagues, I suppose. For the dead. For the future." He paused again. "That's why he was here—Spinner. To talk about what we do next. Fifteen years ago we took a stand, and we've been living with the consequences ever since. Back then we all agreed to stay away from each other, for safety's sake. But now they've found Spinner, he's worried we're all in danger—and the research is too."

"Do you agree with him?" Annalie asked, worried. "*Are* you in danger?"

"Spinner's got a world of trouble after him, and some of the others are hanging in the wind. But I should be okay. I've got an island full of pirates to protect me. As long as the Kangs think I'm worth more to them here than I would be if they handed me over for a reward, then I'm safe."

"Bet the Admiralty pays a good reward," Pod observed.

"Good weather information is worth its weight in gold," Gari said stiffly, "and it's the gift that keeps on giving. They can only sell me to the Admiralty once, but they'll always need someone to tell them about the weather." But even Gari himself didn't seem convinced. "If something does happen to me, I can destroy all the key data to prevent it falling into the wrong hands. But it won't happen. I've got my data in a very secure location. I hope Spinner has too."

Annalie gave him an uneasy smile. Spinner's secrets were stored on the *Sunfish*, hidden where they'd always been inside the doll Spinner had made for Annalie when she was a little girl. She was not at all confident that that counted as a secure location.

"So, do you know where Spinner's going next?" Annalie asked.

"He's going to see Sujana."

"All the way up north? It's a long trip."

"They're all long trips from here," Gari said.

"Is he still traveling with the Kangs?"

"He shipped out with them. I didn't discuss his itinerary in detail."

"If he's still with them, is there a way we can get a message to him?" Annalie asked hopefully. "The Kangs must have a way of making contact, even when they're at sea."

"Call Spinner!" Graham chimed in. "Bad Spinner leave Graham behind."

"I don't think they'd let you do that," Gari said.

"But surely, if *you* asked them—"

"Oh no," Gari said. "I don't think I could. They wouldn't like it."

"Aren't you their number one weather guy?" Pod said. "That ought to give you some pull."

"Well, yes, and no," Gari said haughtily. "I wouldn't want to annoy them."

Annalie looked at him in frustration. "Well, did the two of you discuss how you'd get in touch with each other if you ever needed to?"

"We decided it was safer to continue silent running. It's worked pretty well up till now."

"So, you have absolutely no way to contact him?" Gari shook his head.

"Is there any way he can contact you?" Gari shrugged.

"Well, could you at least let me use your link network?"

They knew the pirates had to be able to access the links from the island, but their access was heavily protected.

"Oh no, absolutely not," Gari said. "You have to have special clearance to use it."

"Don't you have special clearance?"

"Well, of course. But *you* don't."

"All I want to do is send a message to Spinner!" Annalie said, frustrated almost beyond endurance.

"They monitor my transmissions. At least I think they do. They *can,* if they want to. I would, if I were them. Anyway, if I let you use my code to send a message, they'd be furious."

"I'd let you check it first."

"But how would I know it wasn't some secret code?" Gari said. "You could be messaging anybody. It might not really be Spinner. Somebody may be monitoring his transmissions, it could be intercepted, they could track the message back here, to me and this island! There are too many variables. It's too dangerous."

"But you know Spinner, you know who I am," Annalie protested. After all he'd told them, this late outbreak of paranoia made no sense to her. "Can't I just send him a simple message telling him we're coming?"

"No. I'm sorry. No."

Annalie could have wept with disappointment but she tried to remain polite. "Well, thanks anyway," she said. "You've been very helpful."

Currents

"Danny Boy always a mean grump," Graham said when they were back in their quarters.

"All he had to do was send one message," Annalie said, "and he wouldn't even do that."

"He's scared," Pod said. "He lives with pirates. They're paranoid. Decide they can't trust you, you're done."

"It would have been so simple. One sentence. One short sentence."

"It's okay," Pod said. "We know where he's going. We've just got to keep our heads down while they fix our boat, and then we can find the others and get out of here."

"I wish there was more we could do," Annalie said. "It's so frustrating to think we're just going to be sitting here wasting time when we could be out looking for Will and Essie."

"You heard Wirehead," Pod said gloomily. "They're not going to give us a boat."

"He did say he'd put the word out," Annalie said, trying to decide how much faith to put in Wirehead's promise. "You think he will?"

"They've got plenty of boats," Pod said. "They're all probably out and about, shaking people down all over the place. You know: 'Hello local fisherman, where's my protection money? And, by the way, have you seen any lost kids in life jackets?'"

Annalie smiled. "Maybe we should offer a reward."

"Might have to rob the Admiralty again to do that."

"I don't think I could do that again. It's the most terrifying thing I've ever done," Annalie said.

"You didn't seem scared. When you were talking to that officer you were just ice cold," Pod said with admiration.

"I got lucky," Annalie said. "I guessed things were pretty much the same on every base, and it looks like I was right."

Pod looked at her quizzically. "So—you were in the Admiralty for a while?"

"Not exactly. It was an Admiralty boarding school," Annalie said, faintly embarrassed. "Triumph College."

"An Admiralty school? Serious? Why'd you go there?"

"Spinner wanted me to go. If you want to go to university you have to go somewhere like that. It doesn't have to be Admiralty, but it helps."

"What's university?"

"It's where you go to learn how to be a doctor or a scientist or an engineer."

"Which you gonna be?"

"I have no idea. Anyway, it's never going to happen now."

"Why not?"

"How can I go back and join the Admiralty now, after all we know about them?" Annalie said.

Pod looked at her, frowning, trying to make sense of it all. "But your dad wanted you to go there, right?"

Annalie nodded.

"So, *he* must've thought it was a good idea."

"I guess he did," Annalie said.

"Was it a good school?"

"It's supposed to be the best," Annalie said with a sigh. "Can't say I liked it very much. I didn't really fit in there."

"I never went to school," Pod said thoughtfully. "I thought maybe one day I'd like to go." He glanced at her shyly, and looked away again, embarrassed. "But it's probably too late now."

"I'm sure it's not," Annalie said. "But do you really want to go to school?"

"I can't read like all you guys," Pod said.

"Oh," Annalie said. "Sorry. Yes. I forgot." She paused. "I could try and teach you, if you like."

"Yeah. Thanks." Pod gave her a slightly embarrassed smile. "I thought maybe one day, after we've found the others and your dad, I can look for my sister and get her back. Then I'll get a job, and we can go to school, her and me. She's younger than me, so she's got more of a chance."

"I promise we'll help you find your sister," Annalie said.

"Thanks," Pod said. "Right after we find Will, Essie, and your dad."

Annalie laughed, and then her laugh went wobbly. "I really miss them," she said.

"I know," Pod said. "Me too."

"I keep hoping some boat's going to come in and they'll be on it."

"It could still happen."

"But what if it doesn't?" Annalie said. "What if they washed up somewhere, and they're hurt, and they're waiting for someone to rescue them? Or they found another bunch of cannibals?"

"We don't know what happened," Pod said. "Maybe some boat picked them up that was going the other way. Maybe they ended up in a port on some other island. They could be waiting for us to come and pick them up right now."

"You're right," Annalie said, trying to remain positive. "And even though we can't leave yet, we can still try to join the links, in case they *have* sent us a message."

"Who you going to ask? Wirehead? He'll make you pay extra for it."

"No, not Wirehead," Annalie said.

"I already told you," Gari said huffily, "I can't let you send any messages."

"But I don't want to *send* a message," Annalie explained patiently. "I just want to *check* my messages, to see if I've got any. It's very important."

"What's so important, anyway?"

"We were traveling with my brother and my best friend," Annalie said. "We got caught up in that big storm a week or so ago—that's when our mast got snapped—and Will and Essie got washed overboard. We tried to find them but we couldn't, and we're hoping that a boat might've found them and picked them up. If they did, they might've sent us a message."

"Statistically speaking, it's very unlikely they got picked up by another vessel," Gari said in his abrupt, insensitive way.

Annalie's eyes prickled with tears, but she said, "Is it really so unlikely, though?" She turned to look at his enormous array of monitors, charts and readouts. If anyone knew how to find Will and Essie, it was him. "If I showed you where we were when the storm hit, do you think you could tell me whether it was likely someone else ran into them?"

"You know what your position was?" Gari asked, sounding surprised.

"Yes, I do," Annalie said. She had brought the charts with her, just in case, and now she spread them out in front of him. "We were about here when the storm hit," she said, pointing, "and we ended up here. Do you know if many boats go through here? Do your people go that way much?"

"My people? You mean the Brotherhood? No, they tend to follow a different route. That's a bit of a back-water." He paused, still studying her chart. "What's all this?" he asked, pointing to the crosshatched areas.

"That's where we went back to look for them," Annalie said. "We thought—"

"Well, you thought wrong," Gari said. He swiveled to his keyboard and tapped away. Displays popped up—charts filled with swirling lines and curving arrows. "There are strong currents flowing through that water. See?" He indicated the swirls and arrows. "If your friends were washed overboard, it's unlikely they stayed where they were."

"So where does the current go?" Annalie asked.

Gari turned from his screens to Annalie's chart. He picked up a pen and drew a curving line which went in quite a different direction from their search area. "There," he said.

"We were looking in the wrong place the whole time," Annalie murmured, dismayed.

"You were just thinking about the wind, weren't you?" Gari said rather patronizingly. "You've always got to consider the currents as well."

"I know, but—," Annalie began. This time the tears did begin to flow. "We wasted all that time," she said.

"Well, you weren't to know," Gari said, deeply uncomfortable about having a crying girl in his office. "If you're lucky, they might have washed up here." He pointed to some tiny islands at the bottom of the chart.

"You think they could be there?"

"If they're anywhere," Gari said. "But it's a long shot."

Annalie felt a surge of fresh hope. "It's better than nothing," she said, wiping her eyes with the back of her hand. "Thank you. You've been a huge help."

Dan Gari looked pleased. "If you like," he said, a visible struggle crossing his face, "we can check your shell for messages."

"Really?"

"But you can't send any. And I'm deleting the access code afterward."

"That's okay," Annalie said.

She handed him her shell. He turned away from her, entered a code, and then handed it back. She waited, holding her breath, but no messages arrived.

"Nothing," she said sadly, and handed the shell back to him so he could delete the code again.

"They're not likely to have been picked up round there," Gari said. "Big boats have no reason to go that way and local boats tend to avoid it because of the current. But a lot of stuff washes up on those islands. Maybe your brother and your friend did too."

Rafting

Sailing a raft was very different from sailing the *Sunfish*. It rode very low on the water, and when waves washed over it, Will and Essie got wet. The *Sunfish* had two masts, a number of different sails, an engine for those times when the wind was not obliging, and it had been designed to be steered. The raft had a single sail and had been built only to float; although it had a rudder, it was not really much use, and they soon found that the currents had as much power over it as the wind. They drifted, slowly, out to sea, with no real notion of where they were going. Will hoped the wind and the current would keep them traveling in a more or less easterly direction, and that this might take them somewhere in the vicinity of Dasto Puri.

They drifted for a day, a second day, a third day. The sky was blue and cloudless; nothing crossed their path and they saw no sign of land. Fish began to follow the boat; Will caught two: they ate one and hung up the other to dry. They saw the occasional seagull and Essie managed to hit one with the slingshot. It plummeted out of the sky and hit the water with a splash. Will leaped in after it and swam to retrieve it like a hunting dog, making Essie laugh. He fretted about the slow progress they were making, but there was nothing to be done about it. They couldn't make the wind blow any harder or the currents pull them along any faster. For three whole days, things were dull but tranquil.

On the fourth day, they saw a shape on the horizon. Will spotted it first. "There's something there!"

"Is it a ship?"

"A container ship. A big one!"

"Where'd we put the kite?"

The kite had been Will's idea. They had no signal flares for alerting a passing vessel to their presence, but Will thought if they could send up a kite with a message on it—HELP!—they might be able to attract someone's attention. They'd made the kite as large and colorful as they could, and they'd tested it back on the island to make sure that it actually flew.

The only thing they hadn't counted on was the wind. On the island the wind had seemed to blow constantly, at least on one shore; now, out here in the ocean when it actually mattered, the wind had slackened. The sail hung limp. The kite would not fly, no matter how hard they tried. The two of them jumped and shrieked and waved their orange life jackets, they tried signaling with pieces of glass, they did everything they could think of to attract attention, short of actually setting the raft on fire. But the container ship slid across the horizon, imperturbable and distant, and passed away without ever turning in their direction.

"Why didn't they see us?" Essie wailed.

"Weren't looking," Will said glumly. "Big boats, tiny crews."

"There'll be another one along, right? Where there's one, there'll be more?"

"Yeah," Will said. "For sure."

But there weren't. More days passed. No other ships came by, even at a distance. There were no rocks, no islands, no land. Only glinting sea and cloudless sky and the occasional fish, which they did their best to catch.

Then the wind changed. A storm front gathered on the horizon, then rolled toward them. Watching it approach, Will took down the sail while Essie did her best to secure anything that wasn't already tied down in preparation for what was to come.

Soon it was upon them: gusting wind, sheets of rain, and a choppy white-capped swell. As storms went, it was not a particularly bad one; and if they'd been on the *Sunfish,* they would have ridden it out quite happily sitting in the saloon, keeping out of the rain, and playing old card games. But in an open raft, it was entirely another story. Each wave that washed over the raft smashed into their belongings, which were lashed down with whatever fixings they'd been able to improvise: old bits of rope, plaited cords made from plant fibers or bits of junk. The wind blew and the waves scoured and the raft rocked and tipped, and all too soon their fixings began to give way. A particularly large wave came tumbling over them; with a snap, a strap gave way and a whole section of equipment came loose; precious fishing gear spread across the raft; Essie and Will pounced, trying to gather up as much of it as they could, but the fishing net, the reel, a large water container, and a spare piece of rope went overboard. Will let out a despairing cry as his precious fishing gear vanished into the water, and Essie had to grab him by the legs to prevent him from jumping in after it. He managed to claw back the floating container and he almost snagged the fishing reel, which taunted him by floating for a moment or two, just out of reach, before sinking into the churn.

"Let's try and tie down the rest of it," Essie said.

Will seemed stunned by the loss of his fishing gear and for long moments he couldn't move, staring into the water as the wind whipped around him. Essie did her best to secure everything she'd managed to save from the broken bundle, rewrapping and retying, before giving up and settling in with her arms around the mast and the remaining gear in case anything else terrible happened.

Nothing did, although it certainly wasn't pleasant; the wind lashed them for another hour or two; then the storm rolled away as swiftly as it had come. They were left, sopping, without fishing gear, although with a supply of fresh rainwater.

"We'll be okay," Essie said gamely. "We've still got supplies. And we're sure to find help soon."

Will said nothing. He was already trying to think of ways to trap fish (or birds, or anything, really) without any gear.

More days passed, still without sight of land or other ships. Their supplies dwindled and they began to get scared. Neither of them really wanted to voice their fears to the other, but at last Essie said it: "What happens when our supplies run out?"

"Something will come along," Will said. "We'll catch something. It'll be okay." He paused. "At least we can still make fresh water. You can survive quite a long time without food, as long as you've got water."

Essie did not find this thought very comforting, but she did her best to rally their spirits. "When we reach land," she said, "what's the first thing you're going to eat?"

"A hamburger," Will said instantly, "with two burgers and lots of cheese and tons of ketchup and mayo."

"I want a huge bowl of fried noodles," Essie said, "with spicy chicken and three kinds of sauce and all the trimmings."

"And chocolate cake," Will said.

"And ice-cream with fudge sauce and honeycomb bits and marshmallows on top."

They found they could talk about food for hours, refining their perfect post-rescue menu, discussing the pros and cons of almost every kind of junk food and sweet treat. It couldn't make them any hungrier than they already were, and it gave them something to think about that wasn't the grim reality of their situation.

But then finally the day came when there was no food left at all. The ocean shimmered around them, flat, empty. "There'll be fish eventually," Will said. "I know I can get something."

But by now they both knew that was not looking likely.

That night they slept as they always did—lightly and uncomfortably—and in the dying hours of the night something woke them: a strange sound, a nickering, clicking, whistling sound.

"What is that?" Essie hissed, drawing herself as far from the edge of the raft as she could. There was no moon, but starlight glowed.

"Dolphins," Will said.

He sat up to see a pod of dolphins moving around the raft. They seemed to be surging insistently around the port side, then turning to look at him directly—were they trying to catch his eye?—before leaping and curving and swimming about again.

"What are they doing?" Essie asked.

"I don't know," Will said.

The longer he looked, the more he realized they were staying in front of the raft's leading edge. He'd taken the sail down for the night, but there was still a current carrying them forward, and the dolphins were swirling about directly in the path of the raft.

"I wish they wouldn't swim right in front of us like that," Essie said. "They're so beautiful. I'd hate to hit one of them."

"We won't hit them, they're too smart for that," Will said. "They like to surf bow waves." He'd seen dolphins surfing the *Sunfish's* bow wave, all exuberance and pleasure in the water. But this was something different.

He pulled himself to his feet and looked ahead. The ocean was a black mirror in every direction with only the faintest shimmer of starlight on its surface—except for directly ahead, where he could see white foam.

"There are rocks ahead!" he cried.

They sprang into action to fend the raft off whatever lay ahead. Will raised the sail and Essie took the rudder, taking their cues from the dolphins, who seemed to think they ought to turn to starboard. Breeze filled the sail. Will grabbed the oar and paddled as hard as he could. Ever so slowly, the raft changed course. The white foam ahead of them drew closer and closer. The raft drifted on in its slow, ponderous fashion, turning past the white water and the rocks that lay beneath it just in time, and floating safely into open water once more.

The dolphins swam with them until the danger had passed, and then went arching away without so much as a farewell squeak or backward glance. Essie and Will watched them go, stunned by what had just happened.

"Did they just rescue us?" Essie asked.

"Looks like it," Will said. "You hear stories about stuff like that happening, but I never really believed it."

The first light of dawn was creeping into the sky now. They could see what they'd nearly hit: a rocky islet, entirely bare of soil or vegetation or shelter of any kind. Just rocks in the ocean.

But where there were rocks there were sometimes fish, so Will spent the morning on his belly, leaning out over the water, hoping he might catch something, but came up empty-handed.

Giving up at last, he slumped down beside Essie. "I'm so tired," he said.

"That rowing looked like hard work," Essie agreed.

He was silent for a moment, his eyes closed. "I don't know how much longer I can keep this up," he admitted.

"Hey," Essie said. "We're going to be okay. You didn't catch anything today, but I know you will soon. Here, have some water. It'll help."

Will had some water. It didn't really help. His reserves of strength were ebbing away; paddling the raft away from the rocks had used up almost everything he had. He knew he didn't have many more efforts like that left in him.

Late in the day, he was woken from a doze by a splash. He looked up; a sleek dark-gray head was looking at him from the water. It let out a little stream of clicks and chirps, and he was about to say, "Hey, the dolphins are back!" when a voice came, seemingly out of nowhere.

"Are you lost?"

Pilot program

Will stared at the dolphin. The dolphin stared back. Then it whistled again and the voice spoke. "Are you lost?"

The dolphin's mouth wasn't moving, but he noticed the dolphin was wearing a harness around its neck. He realized the dolphin must be speaking through some kind of translator unit attached to the harness. They'd encountered this kind of thing once before, on the island of the great red apes; before the Flood, scientists had given the apes translator units that allowed them to turn their thoughts into human speech. They'd used it to create epic poetry.

"Yes, we are," Essie said eagerly. "Can you help us?"

"Where do you want to go?" asked the dolphin.

"Dasto Puri," Will said.

As soon as he said it, he knew it was a ridiculous suggestion. How would a dolphin even know the human name of an island, let alone where to find it? The dolphin disappeared below the water, and for a moment Will thought it had merely swum away. But then he heard clicks and trills and realized that there were more of the pod here, and that they were, perhaps, conferring with each other.

The dolphin appeared again. "You're going the wrong way," it said. "Come."

Will did his best to steer the raft and go where the pod wanted them to go. From time to time, some of the pod would break off and go away to do something else, returning hours later, but at least one dolphin would always remain with the raft, showing them which way to go.

Late on the first day, they saw something that surprised them. Two dolphins surfaced near them; one was wearing a translator, but as they watched, it slipped out of the harness and the other slipped smoothly into it.

The second dolphin then swam up to them. "This is not a very good boat," it said.

"It's a raft," Will said. "It was the best we could do."

"We were marooned on an island," Essie added. "Which island?"

"We don't know its name." Will described it—its shape, the junk-catching spur, the currents—and the dolphin whistled.

"I know that island. Why did you leave? You could die out here."

"I'm trying to find my sister."

"Sister? Family. Families are important."

"Do you mind if I ask you something?" Will said. "Who helped you to talk?"

"We could always talk," the dolphin said. "You just couldn't understand us."

"True," Will said. "But someone gave you that device. Who was it?"

The dolphin let out a long string of sounds and some of the other dolphins joined in before more words emerged in Duxish. "You call them the Admiralty."

"Really?" Will said, surprised. "I didn't know they did this kind of stuff." Teaching animals to talk seemed like a strictly pre-Flood scheme. Graham was a product of the same technological fad—he had a language chip in his head, although he spoke with his own voice.

"After they broke the ocean, they needed our help to understand it," the dolphin explained.

"Understand it how?" Essie asked.

"They wanted us to help them make maps. Navigate. Work out where everything is now that the ocean is different. They captured us and trained us and gave us these word machines. We were part of a pilot program. They wanted us to be pilots. But we didn't want to be pilots. So we left."

Will looked at the dolphin in delight. "You mean you ran away from the Admiralty and took their tech with you? That's awesome."

The dolphin had a particularly roguish look on its always-smiling face. "It's not so hard to escape. It's a big ocean. Especially since you broke it. It's bigger than it was before."

"You know we didn't do that personally, right?" Will said nervously.

"What's done is done," the dolphin said philosophically.

"Well, thank you very much for helping us," Essie said formally. "We really appreciate it."

"It's all right," the dolphin said. "We weren't busy."

The dolphin looked like it was about to swim away. "There is just one more thing," Will said quickly. "Our fishing gear got washed away by a storm, and we're not as good at catching fish as you are."

"Would you like some fish?"

"If that's possible," Will said politely.

The dolphin let out a string of noises, but no more words, and disappeared below the surface. The other dolphins answered, and in a swirl of dorsal fins, the pod went surging away. Will and Essie watched them go anxiously.

"Do you think I offended them?" Will asked.

"I hope not," Essie said.

An hour passed, with no sign of the dolphins. Then Essie spotted a curved fin on the horizon. They stood up to get a better look and saw that the pod was returning. The surface of the water seethed, and it took Will a moment before he realized what he was looking at.

"They're herding fish," he said.

"They're what?"

"They've found a school of fish and they're driving them toward us."

Will was right. The pod cruised through the water, surrounding the school of fish, steering them, frightening them, driving them up to the surface so the smaller fish flapped and leaped in panic. The school came closer and closer to the raft. A few fish leaped out of the water and right onto the raft, and Will and Essie scrambled to grab them as they slithered by. But the dolphins weren't finished. They started slapping the water with their tails, stunning the fish and flicking them nonchalantly onto the boat.

"This is amazing!" Essie said, gathering fish as fast as she could.

Some of the dolphins were tossing individual fish to them with their snouts and bouncing them off their backs, like sportsmen doing their best trick shots.

"They're just showing off now," Will said. And they *were* showing off. But that was one of the things he liked about dolphins: they were cool and they knew it, and they didn't care.

Will and Essie kept collecting the feast of fish, not knowing how long they would need to make it last. The dolphins' presence was miraculous, but it also felt like a whim; Will knew at any moment they might lose interest and swim away again.

Sure enough, as soon as the dolphins had finished swatting fish onto the raft, one of them lobbed up beside them and asked, "Are you *sure* you want to go to Dasto Puri?"

"Yes," Will said. "Why?"

"The people there are not very nice."

"We don't have much choice," Will said. "That's where my sister was headed."

"We don't go to that place anymore," the dolphin said. "They tried to catch us and steal our word machine. We don't like to be captured."

"That's okay," Will said. "You've done enough for us already. We can get there under our own steam."

The dolphin let out a string of clicks and squeals, annoyed that Will was being so slow on the uptake. "If you go there, they'll catch you too."

"Why?" Will asked, alarmed. "Who lives there? Slavers? Pirates?"

"Humans," the dolphin said witheringly. "But I suppose *you* call them pirates. You should go to the volcano island. Dasto Dari. Much nicer people there. Hardly ever erupts."

"But—" Will said.

"That is all. We're going now. Good-bye!"

The dolphin pod pirouetted around the boat, chattering and squeaking, and then all of them dived under the water and vanished, definitively, leaving Will and Essie alone once more.

"Pirates?" Essie said.

The help kite

They drifted for the rest of the day, and all the next, without seeing very much. Then, just as the afternoon sun was sinking below the surface of the sea, Essie saw something.

There was a shape, a small shape, on the horizon. She got to her feet, staring.

"What is it?" Will asked.

"Is that a sail?"

It was.

"Hey!" Essie screamed, waving her arms above her head and jumping up and down, making the raft rock.

"Forget that," Will said. "Paddle!"

Will and Essie both grabbed an oar and began paddling frantically. But the sailing vessel was faster, and it was moving away from them.

"Please don't let us miss them," Will muttered as he paddled.

"The kite!" Essie cried. "Let's try the kite!"

Fortunately, the kite had survived the storm. On her second attempt, Essie managed to get it into the air; it sailed up, tugging against the wind, its colors bright. Essie gazed up at it, hoping with all her heart that the people on board that sailing boat might, just possibly, be looking their way.

"Is anything happening?" she asked.

"They're still moving away from us," Will said.

"They *have* to see it!" Essie said. "They just have to!"

Still the boat sailed on. The sun was already dipping below the water's surface. It wouldn't be long before the daylight was gone and their best chance of rescue would be lost.

"I can't keep up!" Will said, desperate, still paddling.

Essie kept the flag flying. Tears were streaming down her face now at the thought that they had come so close to rescue, only to be left behind again. "Please look," she whispered, tugging on the kite string. "Please!"

"Look!" Will cried. "Are they changing course?"

The boat was turning. Slowly but surely, it began to sail toward them.

Will was still paddling, but then a thought struck him, a thought so surprising he stopped still.

The boat looked strangely familiar.

On it came as the blue dusk descended, like something emerging from a dream.

"Will," Essie said slowly, "is that…?"

Something launched itself from the top of one of the masts and came soaring across the sea toward them, something blue, green, and red. A mighty parrot squawk ripped across the water, and then Graham came wheeling down to drop himself on top of their baggage.

"Where you been?" he said.

Reunited

The four kids and the parrot danced about on the deck of the *Sunfish*, excited and happy and tearful and thrilled, their stories tumbling out of them in an eager jumble.

"We really found you! Both of you! I can't believe it!" Annalie said.

"We both washed ashore on the same island—" Essie said.

"It had this cove that caught sea trash—" Will said.

"And it caught us!" Essie said.

"We thought you must still be on the water, so we looked and looked and couldn't find you—" Annalie said.

"We built a raft, and I made a slingshot, and there were dolphins—" said Essie.

"They said there were pirates on Dasto Puri. Were there pirates?" asked Will.

"Yes, but they helped us," Annalie said.

"Well, sort of," Pod said.

"They made us steal some tech from an Admiralty base to pay for repairs," Annalie said. "The mast, the electrics..."

"Does that include the new paint job?" asked

Will. The *Sunfish*, formerly a sunny yellow, was now painted white.

"It was Pod's idea," Annalie said.

"I liked the yellow," Essie said. "I thought it was pretty. And you never had any trouble spotting which boat was ours."

"Exactly," Pod said.

"We got fake registration papers too," Annalie said.

"*They* were expensive," said Pod.

"We'll need them once we go north."

"North?" questioned Will.

"We found Dan Gari," Annalie said. "We were right: Spinner *is* going to see all the people on the list. He went to Dan Gari first, and now he's gone north to see Sujana."

Will was elated. "I knew it! Did you talk to Spinner?"

"No," Annalie said. "The Kangs wouldn't let me call or send a message. But at least we know where to go next."

"So when did he leave?" Will asked, already on to business. "How much of a headstart has he got?"

"A pretty big one," Annalie said. "But if we're lucky, we can catch up with him."

Will nodded. "Right then. We're going to need some cold-weather gear."

"And more supplies," said Pod.

"Ooh, can we go ashore? Somewhere where there's real food?" Essie begged. "I'm so tired of raw fish I could scream."

"I'm sure we can find some real food," Annalie said. She gave Essie another hug, and then hugged her brother. "I'm so happy to see you both!"

They set a course for a lively port at the north-eastern end of the archipelago, where they used another chunk of the money Essie had borrowed from her father's creditstream to fill the lockers with supplies and buy cold-weather gear. It was always warm in the Moon Islands, so cold-weather clothing was not much in demand, and they got some for a good price. Most importantly, they treated themselves to a huge reunion feast, where Will and Essie ate all the food they'd been dreaming of while they were lost at sea.

Essie got her shell back to find it full of news from home. There was a string of messages from both her father and mother—separately—asking her to come home or send a message or at the very least let them know she was all right. Her father wrote: *Every day I wish I could see you again. If you can't find your own way home, and you want to come back, just let me know, any way you can, and I'll come and get you.*

Her mother, who had a great belief in the power of experts, wrote: *We've got the best people looking for you, darling.*

Will, who was looking over her shoulder, chortled, "They can't be that good!"

"Do you *want* them to find you?" Annalie asked.

"Of course not," Essie said. "I'm sticking with you guys until we finish this thing." But the messages made her feel sad; they reminded her of how far she had drifted from her parents in a relatively short time. At the start of the year, when she'd left for school, her parents had been happily married, and her father was a rich, successful businessman. Now, her father was about to go on trial (any day now, in fact—the trial date had been brought forward) for the collapse of an apartment block designed and built by his company, Tower Corp, and his fortune had been frozen. Her parents' marriage had disintegrated and her mother was now involved with a shipping magnate. (The magnate was building her a house; Essie's mother had sent floor plans and the interior designer's mood boards to show Essie what her new room would look like. Essie was still angry with her mother for betraying her father and would not be bribed, not even with a walk-in wardrobe and a four-poster bed.) And Essie knew that if her parents could have seen her on that island killing seagulls with a slingshot, they would hardly have recognized the daughter they sent off to boarding school just six months earlier. She wrote back to them both, trying to sound reassuring: *I'm okay, I'm happy, please don't worry about me. I'll come home soon.*

Annalie and Will decided to compose one more message of their own, even though they'd had no replies to any of the messages they'd sent. They wrote: *Dear Spinner, we are coming to find you. We know where you're going. If you get this message, please let us know that you're all right, and BE CAREFUL. Graham misses you. Love Annalie and Will*

That done, it was time to weigh anchor once again and embark on the next stage of their journey: to the frozen north.

North

The Moon Islands occupied a great crescent across the southern part of the globe; a large stretch of open ocean lay between the archipelago and the many lands of the northern continent. Sujana Kieferdottar lived in one of the most northerly countries of all. Although spring would be arriving when they got there, it would still be very cold.

It would be a different kind of sailing from now on; they were leaving behind the wild waters of the archipelago with its pirates, cannibals, reefs, and currents, and heading into the civilized world of the north. There, the Admiralty would pose the greatest risk. Their names, their faces, their vessel would all be on watchlists, and a new coat of paint for the *Sunfish* might not be enough of a disguise. It would only take one sharp-eyed sailor on an Admiralty patrol boat, one cautious harbormaster checking a list, and a message would be fired off to Beckett: *I've seen them. They're here.*

And then Beckett would be coming for them.

Avery Beckett was their nemesis: once Spinner's friend and colleague, he was now part of the Admiralty's Department of Scientific Inquiry & Special Projects, which seemed to exist primarily in order to hunt down Spinner and his friends. He had already crossed paths with Will and Annalie several times, and come close to capturing them both. So far, they'd managed to escape him, but their luck could not hold forever.

They sailed through the open ocean for some weeks, never seeing another vessel. The winds were mostly in their favor, and they took care with their water and their rations so they would need to put in to port as infrequently as possible. As they traveled north, the sea and air and sky changed around them; the warm, soft air of the south gradually cooled and sharpened. The wind grew teeth and the ocean turned darker. The nights were cold now.

One day, Pod shouted to them from the deck. "What *is* that?" he cried.

A huge object, brilliant blue and carved into a strange organic shape, was floating off their starboard bow.

"That's an iceberg," Will said.

"An iceberg," Pod repeated, gazing at it in amazement. He'd never seen such a thing. Annalie couldn't tell whether he'd even heard of one.

"Now we're really in the north," Will said.

The coast of Norlind rose up before them: dark, craggy, rising up to mountainous peaks dusted with snow.

For the first time in many weeks, Essie's shell chimed—they were in range of the links again. As the Sunfish cruised toward the shore, Essie read all her messages, then began idly looking through her newsfeeds. A headline caught her eye; she linked to it, and began to read with growing horror.

KANG STRONGHOLD SMASHED

The Admiralty has struck a major blow in the fight against international piracy with the destruction of a Kang Brotherhood stronghold on the remote island of Dasto Puri, in the Moon Islands.

"Following new intelligence, we were able to locate one of the Kangs' most important bases in the Moon Islands and destroy it," said an Admiralty spokesman. "This base was an important center for all their criminal operations in the south, and we believe we've struck a real blow at the heart of this criminal enterprise. They'll find it difficult to recover."

The Kang Brotherhood are known to be involved in a range of serious crimes, including attacks on ships and the theft of their cargoes, kidnapping, the international trade in stolen weapons and technology, smuggling, and people smuggling, as well as a range of other violent offenses.

"We will continue to fight piracy on the high seas for as long as we encounter it and do everything in our power to smash the pirates and secure the safety of the waters for all," the spokesman said.

Two photos accompanied the article. One showed the Kang fleet burning merrily in the foreground, while the town that climbed the cliff burned in the background. At the very top you could just see Dan Gari's tower, also burning.

"It's all gone," Annalie said.

"There were a lot of people on that island," Pod said. "What do you suppose they did with them all?"

"Probably arrested them," Essie said.

"Even the kids?" Pod said.

"It's not like any of them can stay there now," Will said. "There's nothing left of the place."

"No," said Annalie. She hadn't especially enjoyed her time on Dasto Puri, but the Kangs had treated them decently enough once they'd paid their way. It was horrible to think of all those people's homes going up in flames. Had they had a chance to rescue anything before it all went? The marines probably emptied the town and then sent in the flamethrowers, *whoomph*.

"There's another photo," Essie said.

The second photo, presumably taken before the town was set on fire, had been taken on the docks, and showed picturesquely dressed Kangs in handcuffs, fighting and snarling as they were taken to an Admiralty patrol ship.

"Can you make it bigger?" Annalie asked, leaning in to look closer.

Essie expanded the photo as big as it could go.

"Look!" Annalie said. Behind the foreground pirates, other figures were visible. One, a portly shape in shorts and a novelty T-shirt, hands pinned behind his back, had been caught with his mouth agape. Was he roaring in fear? Protest? Despair?

"That's Dan Gari," Pod said.

130

"They got him," Annalie said, dismayed.

"And his research?" asked Will.

"He did say he had a plan to keep it safe," Pod said.

"I bet he didn't get a chance to put it into action," Will said. "It looks like they were all caught by surprise, him and the Kangs. This is bad. Very bad. Did he know where we're going?"

"Yes," Annalie said.

"Do you think he'd give us up?" Will asked.

"I don't think he'd *want* to," Annalie said uncertainly.

"But he's not exactly a tough guy," Pod said. "If they put pressure on him..."

Essie was still looking at the photo. "Hey, is that who I think it is?"

Behind Dan Gari was another figure, tall and male, dressed in black. His image was blurred by movement and his face was turned away from the camera, but there was no mistaking the barrel chest, the shape of the jacket.

Will and Annalie looked closer.

"It's Beckett," Annalie said. "He was there, at Dasto Puri."

"He only missed you by a matter of days," Essie said.

For a moment they were all silent, looking at each other. "What do we do?" Annalie asked finally. "Do we keep going, knowing he could be coming after us?"

"What choice have we got?" Will said. "We still have to find Spinner. We'll just have to try and stay ahead of Beckett."

Sujana

Norlind had never been a populous country, even before the Flood. It was very far to the north and buried in ice in the winter. It had a long, crinkly, folded coastline with a lot of coastal towns that the Flood had simply washed away, leaving only a few lonely spires and bell towers behind. But Norlind also had a central spine of mountains, the northernmost end of a great mountain range that ran through three or four different countries, and there were several large towns and cities nestled on the lower slopes of the mountains.

Sujana Kieferdottar did not live in any of these, however. Her home lay farther up, high on a mountain pass which had once led to a glacier, when there still were glaciers, far away from anywhere. The address Spinner had for her was not even an address precisely: she lived near, but not in, a village so small it took Essie quite some time to even locate it on the links.

The remoteness of Sujana's house presented them with a problem: Did they all travel together up the mountain? Or did they leave someone behind to watch over the boat?

"I don't want to split up again," Essie said.

"But I don't want to leave the boat unprotected," Will said. "What if somebody steals it?"

"This isn't the Moon Islands," Essie said. "There are rules here. People must be able to leave boats unattended, right? Otherwise how would anyone with a boat ever get anything done?"

"True," Will said, "but if you want to keep your boat safe in harbor, you need to have papers and register with the harbormaster, and we'd rather keep a lower profile than that."

"I definitely think we need to avoid anything too official," Annalie said.

"Someone needs to stay with the boat then," Will said, looking around at the others. "I can do it."

"You can't stay here," Essie said. "You *have* to go up the mountain. What if Spinner's there?"

"I'll stay," Pod said.

"Are you sure?" Annalie asked, relieved.

"I can protect the boat," Pod said.

"Graham protect Pod," Graham said, and *skrarked*.

They agreed Essie would accompany Will and Annalie up the mountain. Essie's linking skills might come in handy, and besides, she was the only one who could speak a language other than Dux.

"I don't actually speak Norlind, though," she reminded them.

"But you do speak Hesh," Annalie said. "And Hesh isn't far from here."

"You know they're not the same, right?"

The only way to get there was via three

buses, which were all quite slow and left infrequently. The last of the three buses was an overnight bus. Essie had asked the driver to tell them when they reached the village, but it was so late when they finally got there, and his accent was so thick, it took a moment for her to understand that he was saying, "Kliefenligt!"

They stumbled off the bus into total darkness.

"This is the right place, isn't it?" Will said.

The village slumbered. The stars were bright. It was very, very cold.

Essie flicked open her shell and checked their location. "Yep."

"So, now what?" asked Will.

"According to this, we can pay someone to take us up to the next village, or we can walk."

The darkness and silence were absolute. "I don't see anyone we can ask. Do you?" Will said.

"Looks like we're walking," Annalie said. "But let's wait until the sun comes up."

They searched for somewhere to rest out of the bitter cold. There were not a lot of places to choose from. Eventually they found a largish building with a porch that cut some of the wind.

"We should huddle up," Annalie said. "Share our body heat."

"It's not *that* cold," Will said, embarrassed.

The three of them curled up in the doorway and snatched a few hours' very uncomfortable sleep before the dawn light woke them again.

"I've had worse nights," Will said, sitting up and

rubbing the crick in his neck, "but that would have to be in the top ten."

"I can't feel my toes," Essie said.

"We'll all feel better once we start walking," Annalie said.

"We really won't," Essie said. "*And* I'm starving."

"It's been one night," Annalie teased. "I thought you went six days without food on that raft."

"I'm in civilization now. I shouldn't have to be hungry in civilization," Essie said as they began to walk.

The path led upward, always upward, and their legs soon began to burn. Will was in front, setting a cracking pace; Annalie was next, with Essie trudging in the rear. At first they could see very little; thick mist hung over everything, making it difficult to see more than a few meters in any direction. But then the sun came through the mountain pass and the mist began to melt away. Essie stopped to catch her breath and look around, and she cried out to the others, "Hey, look at this!"

Will and Annalie stopped and turned, and saw that the path they were on emerged from a great soft, billowing sea of pearly cloud.

"It's like we're on another island," Essie said.

"An island in the sky," Annalie said.

"Yeah. Cool. Shall we keep going?" Will was impatient.

They trudged on. The sun kept rising. The mist and cloud burned away and the great vista of Norlind was revealed below them: the mountains falling to foothills, foothills falling to fjords, the distant glimmer of the ocean. Snow still lay in all the hollows, but the land was emerging—bare, dark, ready for the coming of spring.

"Shouldn't we be there by now?" Will asked.

Essie checked her shell. "No signal," she said.

"Typical," Will said, rolling his eyes.

A jingling sound echoed up from below them. Essie heard it first. "Look," she said, "a horse and cart."

It was the sort of thing you'd see on a postcard: a little wooden cart laden with boxes of groceries, colorfully decorated with floral folk art, pulled by a pair of sturdy short-legged horses with bells on their harnesses, driven by a young woman. She reined in her horses as she drew level with them.

The young woman greeted them in Norlind, and Essie replied in Hesh. The woman, hearing her accent, switched to Duxish. "Where are you three going?" she asked.

"Oeferklikken," Essie said.

"Really? Are you sure you haven't made a mistake?" She laughed heartily.

"Do you live in Oeferklikken?" Annalie asked.

"All my life."

"We're looking for someone who lives near the village—she's an old friend of my father's."

The young woman raised her eyebrows. "You mean Sujana?" She poked a thumb at her cart and said, "You'd better hop on."

Papers

Pod was in the saloon playing a board game with Graham. Graham liked playing board games, and he often won. Pod suspected he'd somehow worked out how to cheat at rolling the dice, since he always had suspiciously good luck. Today Pod was slightly ahead and feeling confident about his chances when Graham cocked his head to one side and said, "Engine."

As usual, Graham was right. "You think they're coming toward us?"

Graham gave a non-committal squawk, so they both went up on deck for a look.

A motorboat was coming toward them, an efficient-looking vessel with a big engine and writing on the side. Pod's mouth went dry. He didn't need to be able to read to know who it was.

"It's the police," he said. "What do we do?"

"Stay cool," Graham said. "Be nice."

The motorboat came to a halt at a safe distance and an officer spoke to him through a loudhailer. The words were all in Norlinden.

Trying to hide his panic, Pod called, "Sorry! Don't speak Norlinden! You speak Duxish?"

The officer spoke to him again in Norlinden. His tone was not friendly.

"I'm sorry," Pod called back. "I don't understand."

He had a strong desire to pull up the anchor and try for a quick getaway, but he knew they'd easily outrun him, and he'd just make himself look guilty.

A different voice came over the loudhailer. "Attention vessel. You must identify yourself. How many people on board, please?"

"Just me," Pod called.

"Under maritime regulation 27.3.45a we are authorized to board your vessel. Please move to the railing and keep your hands where we can see them at all times."

Act innocent, Pod reminded himself. *Innocent people don't try to chase the police away or stop them from coming aboard.* "Okay!" he called. "Sure! No problem!"

He stood and watched as the police officers maneuvered closer. Two of them came aboard; a third remained at the controls of the police vessel.

"What is your business in Norlind?" asked the Duxish-speaking officer, who wore a badge on his uniform identifying him as Tomasson.

"Don't have any business," Pod said.

"Then why are you here?"

"I'm just passing through."

"We had a report that you've been anchored here since yesterday."

Pod was surprised. He thought he'd found somewhere ridiculously remote. He hadn't noticed any

138

towns or even houses nearby. "Oh. Yes," he said. "But I'm not staying long. I didn't realize I couldn't stay here."

"It is not forbidden to stay," Tomasson said. "But this is not a designated mooring. If you stay longer than six hours, you must register your vessel with the nearest authority."

"Oh," Pod said. "I didn't know that."

"Who is the owner of this vessel?"

"The owner?" Pod stalled, starting to panic.

"Yes. Who is the owner of this vessel?"

What do I say? Pod wondered, his thoughts whirling. *Do I say Spinner? But I don't know his real name. And he's a wanted man.*

Tomasson was growing suspicious. "I need to see the papers for this boat."

He knew where the papers were but he had no idea whether they'd fool a suspicious Norlinden policeman. "The papers, sure!" he said. "They're below—can I go and get them?"

Tomasson and the other officer conferred, then Tomasson went below with Pod, keeping a wary eye on him as he opened the locker, retrieved the papers, and handed them over. Tomasson glanced over them, then indicated they should go back up on deck. Tomasson gave the papers to the other officer, who scrutinized them closely. The two officers conferred again, and then Tomasson asked, "What is your name?"

"My name?"

Tomasson's eyes narrowed. "Yes. Your name."

Pod's brain had frozen with fear. He could not

possibly give them his real name. He had no identity papers and his name didn't appear on any list. Undocumented people got taken away and put in a camp.

"Will," Pod blurted.

"Will what?"

For a moment he couldn't remember Will and Annalie's surname. "Will Wallace."

"A national of which country?"

"Dux."

The second officer flicked open a shell and began typing. Pod watched anxiously. Will, at least, was a Duxish citixen. He had identity papers. He was on a list somewhere, a real, identifiable person. Pod was a ghost: nameless, numberless, countryless.

Something appeared on the shell. Tomasson and the second officer looked at the report, then looked at Pod; looked at the report, looked at Pod again. With a sinking feeling, Pod realized Will's identity documents probably came with a picture.

"You are not Will Wallace," Tomasson said. "Who are you?"

Variables

Sujana Kieferdottar lived in a tall, narrow wooden house with a steeply sloping roof. It stood all alone, another half an hour's walk above the very tiny village of Oeferklikken. The young woman with the cart was making a delivery to Oeferklikken; she explained that she couldn't take them any closer to Sujana's house because the path was too steep for her horses.

The path was, indeed, very steep, and might have even been too steep for mountain goats. Will, Essie, and Annalie were panting by the time they reached Sujana's front door.

The woman who opened the door was very tall and very wide. Graham had once described her as fat, but she wasn't—she was massive, with broad shoulders, a huge torso, and enormous feet.

"Sujana Kieferdottar?" Annalie asked.

"Yes."

"I'm Annalie, this is Will." She paused. "We're Spinner's kids."

The glower reversed itself into an expression of surprise. "Good gracious. What are you doing here?"

Sujana lived with her elderly mother, who was as tiny and birdlike as her daughter was enormous. The house they shared was like a junk shop, but it also reminded Annalie a little of home, for it was crammed with old things. As soon as you walked in the front door, there were shelves stacked with dozens of pairs of old shoes, tennis rackets and ski goggles, old cameras, suitcases, bicycles and roller skates. Casting a quick appraising eye over it, Annalie thought Spinner might have found a use for some of it, but most of it was the sort of stuff no one would want any more.

"Do come and sit down," Sujana's mother said, wafting them toward the first door on the left. This was a small formal parlor, decorated in a mix of genteel florals (the wallpaper, the furniture, even the rug were all floral, although none of them matched). It smelled of old books and was piled high with still more stuff.

"We can sit in the kitchen," Sujana said.

"But they're company, they should sit in the good room," Sujana's mother fretted.

"We'll be more comfortable in the kitchen," Sujana said firmly. This, too, was piled to the ceiling with old stuff: electric choppers and bread ovens, bits of old tea sets, ancient cookbooks, and very specialized glasses in a myriad of shapes and sizes.

"Have you seen him?" Annalie asked. "Has he been here?"

"Who?" asked Sujana.

"Spinner!"

Sujana paused for what seemed like a longer time than the question required. "No," she said finally.

"Oh," Annalie said, disappointed.

"But Dan Gari said Spinner was on his way here," Will said. "He wants to talk to you."

"Does he?" Sujana said. She turned crossly to her mother, who was clattering baking dishes. "Do you really have to do that?"

"The children look hungry," her mother said with dignity, "and we've nothing in the house."

"I can't imagine what he wants to talk to me about," Sujana said.

"Come on," Will said. "You know what he wants to talk about."

Sujana eyed Will. "Oh," she said finally. "That."

"Spinner's worried you're all in danger," Annalie said.

"What sort of danger?" Sujana asked.

"Beckett," Annalie said. "The Admiralty. They're coming after you."

"He found Spinner," Will said. "He got away, but now he's on the run, and you could be next."

Sujana fingered a mark on the table, not meeting their eyes. "Oh, I don't think we need to worry about Avery."

"Are you kidding?" Will said. "The guy's chased us halfway round the world, threatened us..."

"Threatened you, really? I find that very

hard to believe. Avery wouldn't hurt a fly," Sujana said.

"You reckon?" Will said, looking at Essie and Annalie in surprise.

"I think he's changed a bit since the last time you saw him," Annalie said.

"I doubt that," Sujana murmured.

A baking tray clattered on the bench, giving them all a start. Sujana glared at her mother, who fluttered apologetically.

"I'm sure you've got him all wrong," Sujana said. "To me, he was always one of the good ones. A lot of those Admiralty types don't really get science. They think everything should work to rules and schedules. They like guaranteed outcomes at set times. Science doesn't always work like that—it's unpredictable, it's slow. Beckett was different. He understood that what we were doing was very complex, and had to follow its own rules. He believed in the work, and he believed in us. It was part of his pitch to us, right from the start, when he was putting the team together: this was good work we were doing, important work, the *most* important. Our research was going to save the world."

"He believed that?" Annalie asked.

"Oh yes," Sujana said. "To a certain extent, we all did."

"Wait—you thought rebuilding the Collodius Device was a good idea?" Will said. "After what it did the first time?"

"Yes, but it went *wrong*," Sujana said excitedly. "If it had worked *properly*, the way it was supposed to, we'd be living in an entirely different world today."

"But it did go wrong," Will said. "We can't change that now."

"Yes, but what if we *could* change it?" Sujana said.

"How?" Essie asked.

"Identify the causes. Modify the process. Disrupt the changes. Turn back the clock," Sujana said, her eyes shining.

"Lower the oceans?" Will said skeptically.

"Do you really think that's possible?" Annalie asked.

"Why shouldn't it be possible? We changed the world once. We can change it again. For the better."

Annalie didn't know what to say. To her, this sounded like lunacy.

Sujana's mother slid some delicious warm buns onto the table; biscuits followed. Will and Essie began to eat eagerly but Annalie was too interested in what Sujana had to say to be distracted.

"Avery believed it was possible," Sujana said. "It wasn't just another project for him. Like I said, he was a true believer." Her voice softened as she began to reminisce. "It was so exciting at the start. All of us working together, out in the desert in the middle of nowhere. Site 315, it was called. It was so secret, it didn't even have a name. Boy, that place was lonely. Blazing hot during the day, freezing cold at night. But it felt like we were doing something really important." She sighed. "I don't blame Avery for what happened. He was caught in the middle: he was trying to protect us and our team, but he had to answer to his bosses in the Admiralty. They're the ones I blame. They were in such a *rush*. They wanted it all *now*. But the work wasn't finished. That's why it went wrong the first time."

"You really think that's the only reason it went wrong?" Annalie asked.

"Well, errors in the science, obviously," Sujana said, a little crossly, "but that's because they were rushed into it, too."

Annalie looked at her curiously. "So, if you believed in the project, why did you leave with the others?"

"It was complicated," Sujana said, looking troubled. "At the time it seemed the right thing to do. The Admiralty kept pushing us for results, they wanted us to move on to the next phase, and we were all so afraid of what they were going to do with our work . . . Dan thought they wanted to weaponize it, but he was always so paranoid. And Avery assured us they wouldn't contemplate such a thing. It was *unthinkable*, he said."

"And you believed him?" asked Will.

"Of course," Sujana said, rather offended. "He wouldn't lie to us about something that important."

"What was the next phase?" Annalie asked.

"Rebuilding the device," Sujana said. "The thing is, the device was the easy part. You could build it again tomorrow. It's the modeling that's tricky. That's what I was doing, along with Dan. He worked on the weather, and I worked on the modeling—that's what I do, model complex systems. I try to look at all the variables and then build a computer model so we can understand what the outcomes are likely to be. But when you're talking about water, the atmosphere, the climate—there are so many variables, and everything is interconnected, and one wrong variable can make a big difference to the outcome. So it's painstaking, time-consuming work. You can't rush it." She paused. "I'm still doing the work, you know. I never stopped."

"Dan Gari was still working on it too," Annalie said.

"Was he?" Sujana said. Then she caught what Annalie had said. "Why do you say 'was'?"

"Beckett tracked him down and arrested him," Will said.

Sujana looked stunned. "I don't believe it."

Essie pulled out her shell. There was no service this high up on the mountain, but she was able to retrieve the news article from her shell's memory. She showed it to Sujana, who read the story through, her face registering growing dismay.

"This is why we think Beckett's not such a good guy," Will said. "See that weather tower on fire in the background? That's Dan's tower."

"But those people were pirates," Sujana said, angry and defensive.

"Catching the pirates was just a bonus," Annalie said. "Beckett was looking for Dan Gari, and he found him. That's him, getting arrested. You could be next."

Sujana stared at the photo for another long minute. Then she looked up at them defiantly. "If you take up with pirates, what else can you expect? I'm not in any danger. I haven't done anything wrong."

And she got up abruptly and left the room.

Under arrest

"All right, I'm not Will," Pod said desperately. "I'm just minding the boat for him. But he'll vouch for me—I've got a shell, you can call him on it. It's just below, he'll tell you."

"I need to locate the registered owner of this vessel. Can you help me locate that person?" Tomasson said.

Pod didn't know whose name was on the papers, and he knew he couldn't ask the police to tell him. "I don't know where that person is right now," he said, knowing this didn't help his cause.

Tomasson had clearly had enough. "You need to come with us," he said.

"But what about the boat?" Pod cried. "You can't just leave the boat! I'm supposed to be taking care of it!"

"We will take care of the boat," Tomasson said. "And now you must come with us."

Pod could see no other choice; he ran at the police officers and almost succeeded in flipping one of them over the railing and into the water. Almost—but not quite. Even with Graham swooping in to attack with a screech and a rake of claws, in moments the two policemen had Pod flat on his face on the deck and were busily cuffing his hands together.

"You are under arrest," Tomasson said.

Leaving the second policeman behind on the *Sunfish*, Tomasson and the third officer drove Pod, handcuffed and desperate, to the water police headquarters. Graham had refused to be caught and had therefore been left behind.

"What are you going to do with the boat?" Pod asked. "Where are you taking it?"

"That's not your concern," Tomasson said.

"But what about the parrot? Someone has to look after him."

"We will deal with the parrot."

"Deal with him how?" Pod demanded. "He's a very special bird, very old, very precious to his owner. You're not going to have him put down, are you?"

"We will follow normal procedure regarding the care and control of dangerous animals," Tomasson said.

"He's not dangerous!" Pod cried.

"He attacked us," Tomasson said. "The Animal Control Act states that any animal deemed to be a danger to police or the public will be dealt with in an appropriate manner."

"What does that mean?" Pod asked.

But Tomasson either wasn't sure, or wouldn't say. They took Pod, still cuffed, into the water police headquarters. He tried to stay alert to any possibilities of escape, but as he was escorted through one security door after another, no opportunities presented themselves.

He was taken to an interview room and left locked in there for what seemed like hours. Eventually Tomasson appeared with another colleague. They switched on recording equipment and began to interview him.

"We know you are not Will Wallace. What is your name please?"

"Pod," he said.

"Pod what?"

"Just Pod."

"How old are you, Pod?"

"Not sure exactly. Thirteen."

"Where do you come from?"

"I don't know."

Tomasson gave him a hard look.

"It's true! My parents sold me when I was little. Don't know where I come from."

Tomasson and his colleague exchanged a brief glance, then Tomasson changed tack. "How did you come to be aboard that boat?"

The real story was both complicated and unlikely, so Pod simplified it. "I escaped from the people who owned me, then I met the crew of this boat and they let me stay."

"And where are they now, this crew?"

"They went ashore. They've gone to meet someone."

"Who?"

"Their dad."

"And what is his name?"

Pod had remembered Spinner's real name in the interim, but he still couldn't say it out loud. Spinner's name in a police report was certain to raise flags somewhere. But he couldn't keep saying *I don't know* either.

"Arnold," he lied. "Arnold Wallace."

Tomasson took a moment to check his notes, then looked up at him again. "So, have you had a chance to remember who the boat's registered owner is?"

Pod wished Annalie had told him the answer to this question. It hadn't occurred to either of them that he might be asked. "Look, I don't know whose name is on the papers," he said. "I just know who I've been sailing with. The boat's theirs. You've got my shell, all you have to do is call them. They'll tell you I haven't stolen it."

"Your friends *would* say you hadn't stolen the boat," Tomasson said. "Especially if they'd helped you steal it. So until we can locate the registered owner, you're not going anywhere."

They took him from the interview room to a cell. It was neat and clean, in an orderly Norlinden kind of way, but plain, windowless, and very, very depressing. Pod sank down on the bed, despairing. How was he going to get out of this?

151

When the rain came

Sujana's mother took charge of Will, Annalie, and Essie, making up beds for them in a spare room on one of the upper floors of the tall, narrow house.

"You must have had a long journey to get here," she said. "You're very welcome to stay the night. Perhaps tomorrow Sujana can find a way to contact your father."

"Do you think she could?" Annalie asked eagerly.

"I don't know about these things," Sujana's mother said vaguely. "But I will certainly ask."

Once they were alone again, Will said, "That Sujana was seriously weird."

"I reckon she used to have a crush on Beckett," Essie giggled. "Did you hear the way she talked about him?"

"She definitely had a soft spot for him," Annalie said.

"She's mad," Will said. "Beckett's a psycho. I bet he was always a psycho. But I'm more worried about what's happened to Spinner. He had a huge headstart. Why hasn't he been here?"

Annalie shrugged helplessly. "I have no idea."

"What if we're too late? What if Beckett already caught him?" Will asked.

"We should go down to the village where there's some signal and check the links," Essie said. "Beckett loves splashing his arrests all over the media. If he caught your dad, there's no way he'd be keeping it a secret."

"You're right," Annalie said.

"We should go right now," Will said.

Essie looked out the window. "It's already getting dark. I wouldn't want to get lost on the mountain."

"Tomorrow then," Will said. "First thing."

That night, Sujana's mother cooked dinner for them. The meal was rather strange, and the atmosphere occasionally strained, with Sujana a glowering and largely silent presence.

"I thought you might like to try some Norlinden specialties," the old lady murmured. Norlind was a cold country, and their specialties seemed to include animals that no one in Dux would ever have thought of eating. There was pickled reindeer head, fermented fish served with strange herbs, a strong-smelling greenish cheese and a stew made with rubbery rings of meat of a disturbingly functional nature. ("Do you think that was intestine?" Essie asked later.) The salad was made of moss. Once you got past the unusualness of it, some of it was quite nice, although some of it was really not.

"Norlinden food is an acquired taste," Sujana's mother said, after she'd watched them tackle it with varying degrees of enthusiasm. "Do have some bread."

"I like the food," Will said. "I'm not fussy."

"Of course," the old lady murmured, "it's difficult to get all the old things nowadays."

"Really?" Annalie said politely.

"Oh yes. They have to use different fish, for one thing."

"The old kind are extinct," Sujana explained.

"And the reindeer heads really don't have the depth of flavor any more. They used to hang them for a hundred and eighty days," Sujana's mother mused. "Even the companies that used to make the things I liked don't exist anymore. You can't get Hiffirin's sauces these days. You wouldn't remember them, they were before the Flood. But they were very good. And fruit, too. Fruit is different."

"Mother thinks the fruit used to taste better before the Flood," Sujana said.

"I don't think it, dear. I know it. You don't believe me, but it's true."

"I do believe you," Sujana said. "Fruit responds to the environment it grows in. Change the environment, change the fruit."

"This was my grandmother's house, you know," Sujana's mother said. "I used to stay here in the summertime. It was lovely here then. In summer there were so many alpine flowers. Beautiful." She paused. "Of course, even then, when I was a little girl, long before the Flood, the weather was going wrong. There used to be a glacier up there." She pointed to the roof, indicating the glacier had once been higher up the mountain.

"It vanished, between one summer and the next. One year it was here, the next year it came down, all at once, melted in the spring, just like that. They said it had been there for tens of thousands of years, and then it was gone." She paused. "When the Flood came, I was living by the sea. I had a nice house and I was building a beautiful garden. The first I knew of it was when I heard them talking about a storm in Brundisi. It was a very strange storm, it was on the news, and it started to rain and it didn't stop. At first it seemed like the sort of thing that happened everywhere—strange weather—but then the storm came to Norlind too. It spread everywhere, right around the world. Clouds like you'd never seen before. And then it rained. It rained and rained and rained, so much rain, like being under a waterfall. The land is very steep here. The water ran down the mountains and made flash floods that went through the towns, all the way down to the fjords. Then the ocean rose and took the rest.

"I tried to go to work that day. The authorities had warned us to stay in our homes, but I had an important report to finish. I didn't know, you see, that the world was about to end. So I put on my rain boots and coat and went out into it. The water was everywhere but there were still people trying to go about their business. The streets were choked with cars. No buses were running, no trains. I was walking, getting soaked. I didn't make it to the office, luckily—I probably would have drowned if I had. You couldn't open the windows in my building and the water rose so fast the emergency exits would have been underwater. As I was walking I heard a roar, and then a great surge of water came toward me. I ran into a shopping mall. We were all running up the escalators as the water poured in behind us, fighting up the stairs to get high enough. So much water, so powerful, filled with debris. If it hit you, you went down and you never came back up. I waited in the mall for the rest of the day, and the day after that. We kept hoping someone would come and tell us that it was safe to go out, but no one came. Eventually the water went down a little and a few people started to leave. I decided to go too—I wanted to make sure my little house was all right."

Sujana's mother paused. "The flash flood had burst the back door open and gone right through. Someone had already stolen my valuables and everything was sodden and stinking. I started cleaning up—there was mud stuck to the walls, it was impossible to get it off—but then the police came and told me that the ocean was rising, they didn't know how far it would come, I needed to get to higher ground. So I packed up everything I had left, and I brought it here, to my grandmother's house, and I never went back." She paused. "It all drowned. My lovely house, my garden. The office, the company I worked for, all of it was gone. We sold office supplies. Paperclips. Not much call for paperclips after the sea rose and swallowed everything."

"Not everything," Essie said, trying to offer reassurance, "not forever. The world's been rebuilt."

The old lady gave her a kind smile. "I know, dear," she said. "But not *my* world."

Paperwork

Pod spent a wretched, lonely night in his cell.

The next morning, he was taken out and put in another interview room. A woman came in, looking like she'd stepped out of a whirlwind; her hair was wild, her stockings laddered, and she looked terribly tired.

"So," she said, "they tell me you're undocumented."

"I've got no papers," Pod agreed cautiously.

"I'm Sera, I'm a refugee caseworker," she said. "I'm here to help. You're lucky I had a little gap in my schedule, sometimes it can be weeks before I can get to see people." She opened a handmade felt bag and rummaged inside for some papers. "Now, you don't have a last name or country of origin, is that right?"

"That's right."

"Are you making a claim for asylum here in Norlind?"

"Asylum?"

"Do you want to be allowed to stay here?"

"No," Pod said. "I want them to let me go."

"Right. We won't be needing *that* form then. So. You haven't been charged with anything yet. Something about tracking down the owner of a boat—"

"It's not what they think! I swear I didn't steal the boat—"

"Of course not," Sera said, with an automatic, not-reassuring smile. "If they place charges, you'll probably be kept in custody until the court date comes up. If you're found guilty, depending on the judge, they might put you into juvenile justice or they might just deport you. Oh wait, you don't have a country of origin, do you?"

"No," Pod said.

"Right. Well in that case they'll probably send you to Camp Lov or to Tappa."

"Where?"

"Camp Lov is on an island north of Dormund. It's not bad as camps go, although it is pretty cold in the winter. Tappa is in the Bay of Kinute."

Pod had heard of the Bay of Kinute. "You mean Hulk Harbor?" he said, alarmed. "I'm not going there!"

"I'm afraid you don't get to choose," Sera said. "It's more a question of who will take you."

"Once you're stuck in those places, you never get out," Pod said. "If they don't press charges, what happens to me then?"

"Well, they'll still deport you," Sera said.

"But what if my friends come to claim me?" Pod asked. "We don't want to stay in Norlind. If you just let me get in touch with them, they can vouch for me, we can all get out of your hair, and I won't be Norlind's problem any more."

"But we've already started the paperwork," Sera said, as if that settled everything. "You're in the system

158

now. Even if they don't press charges, something will have to be done. We can't just let you go."

"But I have somewhere to go!" Pod said. "I have friends who'll take care of me!"

"I'm sorry," Sera said. "We have rules."

Pod spent the rest of the day in his cell. Then, precisely twenty-four hours after he was signed in to police custody, Tomasson appeared and unlocked the cell door.

"Have you decided not to press charges?" Pod asked hopefully.

"We're still pursuing our inquiries," Tomasson said. "But you are a juvenile. We can't keep you here longer than twenty-four hours. You're being transferred to a youth shelter."

There was more paperwork, then Tomasson gave Pod a sealed bag and handed him over to Sera, the refugee caseworker. There were no handcuffs for the transfer; Pod wondered whether that was an oversight or another Norlinden regulation.

Tomasson escorted them back through all the security doors, then put Pod into the back of an electric car. The officer and the caseworker spoke briefly in Norlinden, then Sera got into the driver's seat. "I'm taking you to a youth shelter," she explained. "It's a secure facility, but it's nicer than being in a police cell. You'll stay there until we know what's happening with your case."

What was there to say? Pod nodded.

Sera started the engine and began to drive. Pod opened the envelope he'd been given; it contained Annalie's shell. He checked its display for the symbols that meant someone had called, but saw nothing.

"Can I make a call?" he asked.

"Oh!" Sera said. "Did they give that back to you? Yes, I suppose you can."

He called Essie's phone, already rehearsing in his mind what he was going to say. The phone rang and rang, then he heard a click, and he jumped in and began to speak: "Essie, tell Annalie—" But then he heard Essie's voice speaking over him, carefree and bright: "Hi, this is Essie, you know what to do!" Then there was a beep. He hesitated, then said, "Guys, I'm in trouble. Call me back!"

He saw the caseworker glance at him in the rearview mirror, and he sank a little lower in his seat.

They were driving through late afternoon traffic. He wondered how far they had to go. "This youth shelter," he said, "how far away is it?"

"Oh, not too far," Sera said vaguely.

Pod looked around him, wondering what to do. She'd said the shelter was a secure facility; this might be his best—indeed, only—chance to escape. The lights turned red and the car came to a stop. He reached out a stealthy hand and tried the door handle. It moved but the door stayed shut—it was locked. He peeped over at the front passenger door, but had no way of telling whether it was locked too.

The lights went green. The car began to move again.

The wait at the traffic lights is quite long, he thought. *If I jump out while she's stuck in traffic, there's nothing she can do about it.*

He waited anxiously for another red light, but the traffic flowed smoothly past green light after green light. He began to be afraid they'd reach their destination without stopping again.

A sound startled him—it was a shell ringing. He checked his own, but it was silent. Sera activated a headpiece (it was a very sober one, not sparkly like Essie's), and began speaking in Norlinden. Pod couldn't understand what she said, but he recognized the tone—anxious, put-upon. She seemed desperate to get off the phone, but the caller would not let her go. A light turned amber ahead of them, then red. She came to a stop, still remonstrating with whoever was on the shell.

Pod grabbed his chance. He launched himself between the two front seats, reaching for the front passenger door. Sera shrieked as he pushed past her. The door didn't move. *Locked!* Quick as a flash, he turned and lunged for the driver's door. To his relief it fell open, slamming into the car next to it. Pod fought his way across Sera's lap, spilled out onto the road, gathered himself up and started to run.

The owner of the car he'd hit with the door started shouting, Sera started shouting, but Pod kept running, weaving through the stream of pedestrians crossing the road, and then putting as much distance between himself and his caseworker as he possibly could. He ran and he ran, without any thought of where he was going. He was in an unknown town in an unfamiliar country and his friends were far away. It didn't matter where he went, as long as he got away.

But he didn't run for long. As soon as it seemed safe, he dropped to a walk. Nothing looked more suspicious than a kid running down a street at top speed. He didn't want to get himself re-arrested. He needed to find somewhere he could hide while he worked out what to do next.

Pieces of the machine

The next morning, Annalie was up before Will and Essie. She crept downstairs without waking them and found Sujana, a large, brooding presence, hunched over a cup of coffee at the kitchen table.

"Good morning," Sujana said, eyeing her uneasily. "Would you like a cup of coffee?" She paused. "Oh yes, Duxish children don't drink coffee, do they?"

Annalie shook her head, and got herself a drink of water.

"Did you know about all this?" Sujana asked. "What Spinner used to do?"

Annalie shook her head.

"He never talked about it? The work, or us?"

"None of it."

Sujana nodded, her fingers tapping agitatedly against her coffee mug. She clearly had something on her mind. "It was Spinner who convinced us all to leave, you know," she said. "Some of us would have stayed, I think. But he talked us all round." She paused. "Back then we all agreed to keep the research safe. In perpetuity, until the world was ready for it. Do you think Spinner still means to keep that promise?"

Sujana was looking at Annalie with an urgent intensity. She wasn't making idle conversation—she really wanted to know the answer.

"He never talked about it," Annalie said, "so I don't know exactly what he thinks. But I know he believes this research is important. That's why he's trying so hard to keep it safe."

"But *is* he trying to keep it safe?" Sujana asked. "Or is he trying to keep it safe from the Admiralty?"

"Isn't that the same thing?"

Sujana was silent for a long moment, frowning. Then she said, "The work I've been doing—it's more than just a job to me. It's been all I think about, night and day, for the last fifteen years." She paused. "When we first stole the research, we decided to encrypt the data to keep it safe, and then divide it all up between us. We each had a piece of it. None of it makes any sense without all the other pieces."

"Like a jigsaw puzzle?"

"More like an engine. If you don't have all the pieces, the thing won't go. Of course, it *isn't* an engine: it's a huge and incredibly complex collection of interconnected research. You have to have all of it, or it's worthless."

Sujana gave her a stern look to make sure she was following. Annalie nodded attentively.

"Since the team split up, I've done my best to carry on with my part of the work, and I've made a great deal of progress. Remarkable progress, under the circumstances. But for it to mean anything, I need to be able to plug it all back in to the original data. Do you see?"

"Yes," Annalie said cautiously. The point seemed clear enough—she just couldn't quite see what it had to do with her.

"I can't let that data be destroyed," Sujana said. "It's too important. I don't just mean important to me. It's important for the world."

"Is anyone talking about destroying the data?" Annalie asked.

"Spinner is," Sujana said, guilt contorting her face. "He *was* here."

Annalie was jolted. "So why did you tell us he wasn't?"

"He wanted to talk about what we do with the research now that the Admiralty are after him," Sujana explained agitatedly. "He was talking about moving it, putting it in a safe place where no one can get at it. He said he had a plan, although he wouldn't tell me what it was. But he said that if Beckett ever caught up with him, he couldn't risk letting it fall into the Admiralty's hands. I think he'd be willing to destroy it, or at least destroy his share—"

"And that would mean destroying all of it, because it's worthless unless it's all there," Annalie said.

"Exactly!" Sujana said, in an anguished tone. "Spinner thought he could stay ahead of the Admiralty, but you know that's impossible. What can one man do with the whole Admiralty on his tail? There's nowhere they can't reach. Look what happened to Dan Gari!"

She paused, fretting, then went on. "After Spinner left here, I was so worried. I'd tried to get him to

165

promise he wouldn't do anything that couldn't be undone, but he wouldn't promise, he just *wouldn't*. So—" Sujana broke off, looking wretched.

"So?" Annalie prompted, an awful feeling creeping through her.

"I called Avery." Seeing Annalie's look of horror, Sujana protested, "I didn't know what else to do. I thought if Avery arrested him quickly and unexpectedly, he could still save the research."

"But—but—isn't that exactly what would force him to destroy the research? If he saw Beckett coming for him?"

"Well—not if they surprised him."

Annalie was so horrified she could barely think. "So—what are you saying? Are we too late? Has Spinner been arrested?"

Sujana shook her head. "They missed him somehow. Avery was very angry. He made me promise that if I heard from Spinner again—or if I saw you— then I'd let him know."

"And have you?" Annalie asked, her voice little more than a squeak.

"No," Sujana said. "Once I actually saw you on my doorstep—" She broke off. "Avery promised me he'd take care of the project and keep all the research safe, and Spinner just *wouldn't*... But when you told me about Dan, I didn't know what to think, or who to trust."

"You can trust Spinner," Annalie said urgently. "This research means just as much to him as it does to you. He'd do anything to protect it. I promise you that."

"Then how could he even consider destroying it?"

Annalie thought quickly. "Think about what could happen if the wrong people got hold of it—the Admiralty. You said it yourself, they don't understand science, they don't understand pure research. They want results, and power, and—and weapons."

"The Collodius Process is not a weapon!"

"*We* understand that," Annalie said. "But do they?"

Sujana didn't reply, but Annalie hoped she was coming round to her point of view. "I know Spinner doesn't want to destroy the research," she continued. "He wants to keep it safe, just like you do. And if you help us get away from here, and avoid Beckett, I promise I'll do everything I can to help him keep it safe."

"But what can any of us do against *them*?" Sujana moaned. "I bet Dan Gari thought he was safe, and now he's rotting in jail—and I'll be next."

"It's not too late," Annalie said. "Get away now, while you still can."

"How can I go on the run?" Sujana said. "You've seen my mother. She's never going to leave this house, and there's no way I could leave her here alone."

Annalie didn't know what to say.

Sujana was silent for a moment more, weighing things up. Then she said, "I think you'd better go. As quick as you can. Get back to your boat. Find Spinner."

Annalie felt a surge of relief wash through her. Sujana was not going to betray them. Her mind began racing ahead, back to the boat, back to sea, on to the next destination. There was no time to lose. They must get on, as fast as they could. "Do you know where he was going?" she asked.

"He wouldn't tell me," Sujana said.

Sujana's mother appeared in the doorway. She looked from Sujana to Annalie and seemed to realize at once what was going on. "I'll make you some food for the journey," she murmured.

"What will you tell Beckett?" Annalie asked.

"Nothing," Sujana said.

"Thank you," Annalie said, knowing that Sujana was, at last, being entirely sincere. But she knew in her heart Sujana could not really be relied upon; she had let Beckett back in. He knew where she lived and what her weaknesses were. He would never let her go; he was ruthless in pursuit of what he wanted, and he would do anything, threaten anything, to get it. However good Sujana's intentions were right now, Annalie knew that when Beckett came back, he would soon find out everything there was to know.

And when he did, Annalie wanted to be nowhere nearby.

As she reached the door, Sujana spoke one last time. "When you see Spinner, tell him I'm sorry."

Annalie nodded, and was gone.

Down the mountain

Will, Annalie, and Essie hurried down the steep slope of the mountain as quickly as they could without actually tripping and rolling all the way to the ocean. When they got into signal range again, Essie's shell began to buzz and vibrate in her pocket. She pulled it out and saw the message from Pod. "Uh-oh."

She put the shell on speaker and they all heard Pod say, "Guys, I'm in trouble. Call me back."

Essie called him back immediately and Pod answered on the first ring.

"What took you so long?" he demanded.

"No signal," Essie said. "What's happened?"

Pod quickly filled them in, and Will and Essie looked at each other in dismay.

"Don't worry," Annalie said. "We're coming to get you."

"*And* the boat," Will said.

"Do you know where you are?" asked Essie. "Can you see any signs?"

"I'm hiding out in a park," Pod said. "Under a tree. It's raining." He paused. "Couldn't read the signs anyway."

"Oh. Of course," Essie said. She thought quickly. "Go out on the street, look for some signs, take some pictures and send them to me. Okay? Do you know how to do that?"

"Okay," Pod said. "Don't go anywhere."

He ended the call and ventured out into the rain.

On top of the mountain, where it was sunny, Annalie, Will and Essie looked at each other. "How are we going to get the boat back?" Essie asked.

"We stole it once before," Will said. "We can do it again."

"That still doesn't seem like a good idea to me," Annalie said.

"You got a better one?"

They waited for Pod to call back. It didn't take long. Soon there were photos pinging into her newsfeed and Essie got to work searching all the names she could see—streets, businesses, buildings, the park he was using as a hide-out—until she managed to work out where he was. She called him back.

"Okay, I've got it," she told him. "Sit tight and stay out of anybody's way. We'll be there as soon as we can."

"I'm sorry," Pod said for the tenth time.

"Don't worry," Will said. "Just keep your head down."

The sweep

Dusk came early in Norlind at this time of year. In the park where Pod had taken shelter it seemed even darker, for, unlike the city streets, the park had no streetlights. The park gates closed at sunset; Pod watched people leave. He was hungry. When all seemed quiet again, he ventured out to see whether he could find any food in the garbage.

He crept out of the trees and was making for the nearest bin when he heard a low whistle behind him. He stopped and turned; a girl's face was looking out at him from the undergrowth. She beckoned to him urgently; he frowned, wondering why she was trying to attract his attention. Then from the corner of his eye he caught a glimpse of movement; an electric vehicle was coming toward him.

He ran to the spot where the girl had been hiding. She had melted back into the shadows, and he joined her, holding his breath, while an electric vehicle went gliding past, very slowly.

When the vehicle was gone he said, "Thanks for the warning."

"I not protect *you*. I protect me. They see you,

171

they sweep," the girl said, gesturing with her hands.

"Sweep what?"

"Park," she said. "Many peoples here."

Pod understood. "And we're not supposed to sleep here?"

She shook her head. "But is good place to hide."

"You don't have any food, do you?" Pod asked.

The girl shook her head. "Sometimes there's soup. I show you. But sometimes dangerous."

"Why is it dangerous?"

"Sometimes police come to soup place. Check papers. Take you away." She looked at him shrewdly. "You got papers?"

He shook his head. "You?"

She smiled and shook her head. "We wait now. Soon, check bins."

Pod nodded. "You don't mind sharing?"

She shrugged.

They settled in to wait.

"I'm Pod."

"Lyope."

"How long have you been here?" Pod asked.

"Norlind? One month. My mother send me. I go to my uncle."

"Does he live here?"

Lyope looked uneasy. "Yes."

"In this park?"

"No. He has house." She paused. "He away just now. I wait for him."

Pod felt a prickle of alarm. "Does he know you're here?"

"My mother send word I coming."

"But do you know if he's coming to get you?"

"He comes," Lyope said, with an uncertain toss of her head. "Eat now?"

They crept out of the trees and hurried over to the bin. Pod had longer arms than Lyope; he reached in and carefully lifted out everything he could put his hands on, laying it out on the footpath for inspection. The pickings were slim: half a sandwich, made rather soggy by something else in the bin; a third of a bottle of drink; an apple core with some fruit still left on it. The rest was empty wrappers, bottles and various unpleasant things. They carefully divided what they'd found and made a meager meal of it, stuffing the rest of it back into the bin.

"Where'd you come from?" Pod asked.

"Camp Lov."

Pod looked at her interestedly. "That's one of the places they were threatening to send me."

"You no go there," Lyope said firmly. "Very bad."

"It's a refugee camp, right? How did you get out?"

"My mother pay big money. I travel in box in ship. We all *so* sick."

Pod nodded sympathetically.

"They drop me in city. Someone help me find my uncle's house. He no there. So now I wait." She paused. "When he comes, I get job, help bring my mother."

"Cost much?" Pod asked.

"Plenty," Lyope said feelingly. "You? Where you from?"

"Nowhere really," Pod said.

"Huh," Lyope said, as if she knew what that meant. "What camp you in?"

"No camp," Pod said. "I was a slave. But then I escaped."

Although it was very dark by now, Pod could see the whiteness of her eyes as they opened wide.

"How you do that?" she said.

"Long story," he said. "But I've got friends I'm traveling with. I'm trying to get back to them, and they're going to get me out of here."

"You not stay Norlind?"

"Why would I want to stay here?"

"You seen it?" she said incredulously. "Norlind *paradise*! So nice, so clean. People so happy. And food—*mm-mmm*!"

"Don't suppose you've had much chance to try any of it yet," Pod said.

"Not much," Lyope agreed. "But I see, through windows. Now I here, I *never* going back."

Later, Lyope showed Pod where to find some cardboard to use as a bed—the ground was very cold—and the right kind of tree to sleep under. This tree had long branches and a wide canopy that drooped down to the ground, making a useful hiding place. Lyope already had a spot there; he made his own bed at a discreet distance from hers, and the two of them soon fell asleep. It was uncomfortable, but Pod had spent most of his life sleeping in uncomfortable places, so it didn't bother him.

In the depths of the night, he was woken by sudden noises—the thrash of foliage, voices shouting. Lyope

174

hissed, "Sweep! Run!" then he heard her scamper off into the darkness. Blinding lights flashed across his eyes and he staggered to his feet and began to run too, with no idea of where he was going.

The darkness was almost impenetrable, but the trees behind him were lit up by what seemed like hundreds of swinging torches. A line of people was trampling through the park, sweeping up any illegals they could find. He was aware of a few other people dashing through the trees around him as the line advanced implacably behind them. He heard a cry as someone was caught; it sounded like a man's voice, and he hoped Lyope had managed to escape. The park, he knew, was big, but the wooded band through the middle was not enormous. Once he burst out onto the other side of it, he would be in open parkland, and all too visible. A tree caught his eye—it looked climbable, and without another thought he went up it, desperately hoping that he could get high enough to escape detection before the line marched through. He could hear the branches rustling as he ascended; he hoped the noise wouldn't be too obvious. The branches grew spindly; he couldn't get any higher, and he clung there in the crown of the tree, watching as the line advanced. Flashlights darted and flickered over the foliage; feet tramped through the long grass; now and then, a cry went up as someone spotted something. Sometimes an officer broke out of the line to give chase; the rest of them formed up again, leaving no gaps, and continued the march. No one thought to look up.

The line passed beneath him and away; for a long time after it had passed he could hear voices and movement, shouts and cries, then he heard the sound of doors slamming, engines starting, vehicles moving. They had swept up the undocumented and the unlucky; anyone who couldn't escape had been arrested and taken away. Silence fell once more over the park. Pod crept back down the tree—the descent somehow more difficult and terrifying than the ascent—and found a place to sleep. But his sleep was full of dreams of being chased and captured, and he was glad when the first light began to appear in the sky the next morning. He hoped he might see Lyope again and offer his help, or at least wish her well; but he didn't see her again.

Finding the *Sunfish*

Annalie, Will, and Essie found their way to the park the next morning. Pod had taken a photo of the place where he'd be waiting for them, and they found him easily enough.

"So, the police have impounded the boat until they can contact the registered owner?" Annalie said, getting down to business.

"I think so," Pod said.

"And if the registered owner comes forward, they'll hand it back?"

"I guess so."

"That's easy then," Annalie said.

"What are you talking about?" Will asked. "We can't just turn up and pretend to be Spinner."

"I'm the registered owner," Annalie said.

"You're *what*?" Will said, outraged.

Annalie explained that while the Kangs were rebirthing the *Sunfish,* they'd asked her whose name they should put on the papers. Naturally enough, she'd given them her own.

"Your name was on the papers the whole time?" Pod said, very annoyed. "I wish you'd told me."

"Why'd you put it in *your* name?" asked Will huffily.

"Spinner is missing and I didn't know where you were," Annalie said. "Obviously we can change it again later."

"But wait a minute," Essie said. "You used your real name? Isn't that going to be on a watchlist too?"

Annalie paused. "Um. Yes."

"If you go and try to claim the boat back, Beckett could be waiting for you," Will said.

"This is all my fault," Pod said glumly.

"Why didn't you get fake papers for yourselves while you were getting fake papers for the boat?" Will said.

"Oh, like it was so easy!" Annalie snapped. "We would have had to do a whole extra mission to pay for that!"

"All right, what's done is done," Essie said, to stop it escalating any further. "Now we need to work out what we do next."

"I say we find out where they've impounded it and just take it back, like I did last time," Will said.

"Too risky," Annalie said.

"What choice do we have?" Will snapped. "You put your real name on the boat. They're going to be looking for you. They're probably waiting for you to show up right now."

"It's not just the boat," Pod reminded him. "There's Graham too. The guy who arrested me was threatening to have him removed. He said he was a dangerous animal."

"Did they catch him?" Annalie asked.

"Not while I was there, but I don't know what happened after that."

Will and Annalie looked at each other worriedly.

"Graham's pretty cluey," Will said. "If he thought he was in danger, he would have just flown away."

"But what if he got lost?" Annalie said.

Graham did have a bit of a knack for getting lost.

"Essie, is there any way you can find out where they might have put the boat?" Annalie asked.

"Let me see what I can find out," Essie said.

It didn't take her long to find the location of the water police headquarters on the map. It was located on a small bay. When they got down there, they discovered that all the impounded boats, including the *Sunfish*, were anchored out in the bay.

"We can't get out there without a boat," Essie said.

"I could swim out," Will said.

"That water's less than ten degrees," Annalie said. "You'd be dead of the cold in minutes."

"We need a dinghy then," Essie said.

"Could we borrow one?" Pod asked delicately.

"You mean steal?" Will said with a grin.

"Can anyone see Graham?" Pod asked.

The four of them studied the boat as carefully as they could in the fading light, but he was not perched in any of his favorite spots above deck.

"Perhaps he's below," Pod said, although he had a bad feeling about it.

"Let's find a dinghy. Then we can go and check," Will said.

They split into pairs and went looking for a dinghy. Annalie and Pod found nothing, but Will and Essie got lucky: Will spotted a kayak. It was hanging from a wall in someone's shed, but the shed was unlocked and the kayak was there for the taking.

The search had eaten up the remains of the afternoon; the sun was gone and the remaining light was fading from the sky. Will and Pod eased the kayak from its pegs on the shed wall and hurried it down to the water's edge as quickly as they could. Will squeezed in and paddled off, leaving the other three to stand there, shivering in the darkness, listening to the splash of Will's paddle growing fainter and fainter. They waited for what felt like a long time. Then, finally, Essie's shell chirped.

"I'm here," Will reported. "There's no sign of Graham."

"Do you think he flew off when they moved the boat?" Annalie suggested, looking at Pod. She'd put Will on speaker. "If he did, he may have gone ashore somewhere near that village."

"He'll be hard to find if he did," Essie said.

"What if the police caught him?" Pod said.

There was a silence. Although Graham certainly *could* have escaped, they all had a horrible feeling that the police probably had him.

"We have to get him back," Pod said.

"But if we go to the police now, they could arrest us," Essie said.

"We wouldn't all go," Annalie said. "Just me."

"How does that make it any better?" Essie wailed.

"Then *you'd* get arrested!"

"I've got the boat—this is our best chance to escape," Will said. "I think you guys should get to the rendezvous point and we should just go."

"And leave Graham?" Pod cried.

Annalie looked at Will. "Pod's right. We can't leave him behind."

Will was silent. He didn't really want to leave Graham behind either.

"We don't even know the police have got him," Essie said. "Maybe he did just fly away. We could sail back to that fjord and see if he's there."

"And what if he's not?" said Will. "Then what?"

Annalie looked at her friends. Essie was wringing her hands. Pod's face had closed like a fist at the prospect of losing Graham.

"I have to go to the police station," Annalie said. "If there's a chance Graham's there, I've got to try and get him back."

The registered owner

"I'd like to report a stolen boat," Annalie said.

The night duty officer moved as slowly as if he were underwater as he reached for his notebook.

"Name of vessel?" he asked in heavily accented Duxish.

"The *Sunfish*," Annalie said.

"Registration? Country of origin?"

Annalie rattled them off.

"Do you have your ship's papers?" the duty officer asked.

"No," Annalie said. "They're on my boat. Which has been stolen. But I have my identity papers."

The duty officer went to a computer and began typing slowly. His eyebrows rose when he saw what came up.

"Oh," he said. "Your boat has been reported as stolen already."

Annalie remembered to look surprised. "What do you mean?"

"Your vessel has been impounded. A person was on board, acting suspiciously. We have been trying to contact the owner of the vessel."

He studied the computer screen and his notes, then he did some slow clicking and typing.

"The owner of the vessel is Annalie Wallace," he read. "What is your name?"

She held her papers up for him. "Annalie Wallace."

He was about to start his laborious typing again, but she interrupted him. "I'm particularly anxious about my pet parrot, who should have been on board the boat. Do you have a record of where he is and what happened to him?"

"A parrot?" the policeman asked, as if she'd asked something perfectly incomprehensible.

"He's a pet and I'm very attached to him. Was he on board when the boat was impounded?"

The duty officer stared at her for another long moment, then went back to his computer, frowning. Tap tap. Frown.

"Yes," he said finally. "A large bird. It's scheduled to be destroyed."

"Destroyed?" Annalie squeaked. "When?"

The duty officer stared, frowned, looked baffled. "Yesterday," he said. "But the paperwork has not been completed."

"What does that mean?" Annalie said. "Does that mean it hasn't been done yet?"

"That would be very irregular," the duty officer said. "But if the order had already been carried out, the paperwork would be here. And it's not here."

"Where was he being kept?" Annalie asked. "Is he still here at the station?"

The duty officer frowned and tapped, tapped

and frowned. "The bird was entered as evidence," he reported finally, "although procedurally, that is not correct. *Procedurally*, the animal should have been passed on to the animal control division." He tapped, tapped, hummed, tapped. "But they have not been this week. So no pick-up was made. Very unusual."

"Does that mean he might still be here somewhere?" Annalie asked. "I have to get him back, I just have to!" She tried to pile some pressure on. "He's a very rare bird and he's very precious to me. I'd hate to think something might have happened to him while he was in your custody."

"Rare?" the officer repeated, looking worried now.

"Very rare," Annalie said. "And valuable, although I don't care about that." She said it in a way that implied that although *she* didn't care, there were others who did care about his value—a lot. And that if the police had unfortunately destroyed a rare and valuable bird, the trouble could go on for eons. "I just want him back. Is there anywhere he could be around the station?"

"I'll check," the duty officer said, and disappeared into the depths of the building.

He was gone for a long time. Annalie waited, fidgeting and anxious. She was almost at the point of bolting out the front door and into the night when the duty officer appeared again through a security door, carrying a large cardboard box. It was taped shut, but as the officer came toward her she saw it bump and jolt, and the officer almost lost his grip on it.

"Graham, is that you?" she cried. "Are you all right?"

184

A flurry of frantic squawking came from inside the box.

"An animal lover among my colleagues," the duty officer said, looking embarrassed by what he had to report. "When animal control didn't come yesterday, he decided to take matters into his own hands. He was intending to find it a good home." He held the box out, and Annalie took it. "You won't mention this to anyone, will you?"

"But what about the anomaly in the paperwork?" Annalie challenged.

"We're going to report the bird as escaped," the duty officer said.

"And that will settle things?"

"We believe it will," the duty officer said.

"Then I'd like to have my boat back now, if you don't mind," Annalie said.

"It won't wait until morning?"

Annalie didn't dare wait that long. "I've already been *significantly delayed*," she said, conjuring up the voice of her most frightening teacher. "I'd like someone to take me to my boat right now."

Flustered by the business of the bird, the duty officer went back to his typing. A form was produced, and Annalie signed it while the duty officer made a phone call.

"This way, please," he said. He came out from behind the police desk and led her out the front door into the cold.

Annalie followed him into the chilly night, her heart pounding, afraid that this could all still go wrong. Graham bumped and thrashed angrily in his box. The walkway down the side of the police station was unlit.

The building loomed on one side of her, a tall wire fence on the other. The walkway was so narrow they had to walk in single file, the duty officer in front, Annalie behind, and it was so dark she couldn't even see where she was putting her feet. They reached the back of the building and came to an open yard where various police vehicles were parked. At the other end of the yard was the police dock and the restless sea.

"That's where you need to go," the duty officer said, pointing to a little office beside the dock. There was a light in the window; someone was on duty.

"Thank you," Annalie said.

"And you won't mention the bird to anyone, will you?"

Muffled swearing came from inside the box. Annalie hoped the officer couldn't hear what Graham was saying.

"I won't," she said.

The duty officer turned and headed back toward his front desk, and Annalie walked across the yard toward the office. She could just make out a couple of police launches tied up at the dock; she guessed another officer had been tasked with taking her out to the *Sunfish*.

She stepped toward the office and was just raising her hand to knock when she heard the murmur of voices from inside. Something made her look through the window. She saw two men. One was dressed in the uniform of the Norlind police; the other, a tall man with a craggy face and a high forehead, was dressed in a black leather jacket and jeans.

She knew him at once. It was Beckett.

Beckett again

Annalie stepped away from the door, her mouth going dry. She hadn't been trying to disguise her footsteps as she approached the office. Was it possible he'd heard her coming?

She scurried away from the office and shrank into the shadow of one of the vehicles. To her horror, the office door opened and Beckett and the second officer appeared in the doorway, looking for her.

Her eyes darted frantically around the yard, looking for a way to escape. The bulk of the police station loomed behind her. On either side of the yard was a huge chain-link fence—she had no chance of climbing that. Ahead was the cold ocean. She imagined making a dash for it, stealing a dinghy from the police dock, trying to escape that way. But even if she could make it past Beckett and the second officer, she knew she couldn't outrun one of the powerful police launches.

Crouching down, she crept along behind the parked vehicles. She would go back the way she'd come. If she could just get out into the street again, she could make a run for it.

Boom! The yard was flooded with light.

The police officer had switched the floodlights on. Dazzled by the sudden glare, Annalie ducked deeper below the cars.

There was nothing to be done. She bolted.

"There!" shouted Beckett.

They were after her.

Annalie fled up the side of the building, now brilliantly lit, the shadows knife-hard. She could hear at least one person hard on her heels, and feared that soon all the police in the building would be pouring out to look for her.

"Stop!" roared Beckett. "You're not getting away from me this time!"

Annalie kept running, but Beckett was fast, horribly fast. She zigzagged out into the street—a car had to swerve not to hit her and honked angrily—but Beckett kept coming. She ran, encumbered by the cardboard box with Graham inside, Beckett's footsteps loud in her ears, more footsteps following. She turned a corner, then another, trying to put some distance between herself and the police station. She felt him swipe for her. His hand closed on her jacket. If she hadn't been carrying the box, she could have wriggled out of the jacket and got free, but she could not let Graham fall. Beckett hauled her roughly back.

"Gotcha," he said with satisfaction. He took the box from her and put it on the ground. Inside, Graham was going berserk.

"You took a big risk coming back for that bird," he said. "I hope he was worth it."

With one hand gripping her tight, he reached into

the pocket of his jacket for his handcuffs. Annalie fought with all her strength to get free, and the handcuffs fell to the ground at Annalie's feet. She kicked them into the gutter.

Beckett glared at her, then twisted her arm behind her back as he reached once more for the cuffs. Annalie heard a faint whistle above her head, then suddenly the pressure on her arm was gone and Beckett staggered forward onto the road.

Annalie turned, astonished, and saw Pod standing there, a long wooden object in his hand. He dropped it with a clatter and picked up the box with Graham in it. "Come on!" he said.

He ran, and Annalie followed, glancing back to see if they were being followed. For a sick moment she feared Pod had actually killed Beckett, but then she saw him stagger to his feet, holding his head. He fumbled in his pocket, this time for his shell. Dazed as he was, she knew he was calling for back-up.

They fled, following the darkest routes through alleys and back streets. They could hear sirens on the move, sometimes close, sometimes far away; the police were looking for them, and the Admiralty would be looking too.

"Here," Pod said. They ran down a quiet street; at the end, the ocean glinted darkly.

"Will's waiting with the boat," Pod explained. "But he can't get in any closer. Getting out there might be a bit unpleasant."

Annalie didn't have enough breath left to ask what he meant.

Pod flashed a signal with a flashlight, and Annalie saw an answering flash over the water. The *Sunfish* was out there with no lights on, invisible in the dark.

They ran to the water's edge. The kayak Will had stolen earlier was lying on the rocks.

"Quick—get in," Pod said.

"But where are you going to go?" Annalie asked.

"I'm going to hang on to the side," Pod said.

"The water's freezing!" Annalie said.

"I'll hang onto the rope, I'll be fine," Pod said. He ripped the tape off the box and set Graham free. "And you can get yourself back to the boat. They're coming. Hurry!"

The sound of sirens was getting louder. Annalie clambered into the kayak.

Pod looped a rope that was attached to the kayak under his armpits. Then he flashed his light one more time as he pushed the kayak into the freezing water, gasping in shock. A winch started up and the kayak gave a jerk, then began to plow through the water, towing Pod behind it.

"Are you all right back there?" she asked anxiously.

"I'm fine," Pod said, although his teeth were already chattering.

Soon the white hull of the *Sunfish* loomed above them, and Essie and Will were there to help them up on deck. The trip had only taken a few minutes, but Pod was already so cold he couldn't move. Will and Annalie had to drag him up.

"Graham, you good?" Pod called through chattering teeth.

Graham fluttered down and landed beside him. "Hate wet," he said, but stroked Pod's cheek with his beak.

While Pod lay on the deck, shuddering with cold, Will and Essie hauled up the sails in double-quick time. The sails filled; the *Sunfish* leaned into the wind and they were away.

A boat race

"That was *not* the plan," Annalie said angrily. "You were all supposed to wait for me to get the boat back."

"We changed the plan," Will said calmly.

"If we hadn't, Beckett would still have you," Pod said.

"But what if someone had seen you?" Annalie said. "You've already escaped from custody once. If they caught you again—"

"They didn't," Pod said, "so stop worrying about it. You got Graham back and we all got away."

"We haven't got away yet," Will said. "We just have to put as much distance between us and Norlind as we can."

Will had set a course west, to get them far away from the shore. Then they would go south. Their last two scientists both lay in a southerly direction; they seemed impossibly far away, but it was too soon to even think about that yet.

They sailed through the night and into the light of dawn.

"No ships on the horizon," Pod reported when it

was light enough to see.

"It doesn't mean they're not out there," Will replied.

All they could do was keep sailing, west and then south. The winds were favorable for a while, but then they shifted. The *Sunfish* slowed, beating against the wind.

"If they're out there, they're going to catch us for sure," Will muttered to Annalie. "Where are we?"

Annalie checked her instruments and did the calculations. "We're out of Norlinden waters," she said.

Not half an hour later, a shape appeared on the horizon. They all took turns looking through the binoculars. There was no question: it was an Admiralty patrol ship.

"Do you think they're coming for us?" asked Essie.

"We'll see," Will said.

He stuck to his course. The others watched the patrol ship as it cruised along on the horizon.

"Are they stalking us?" asked Essie.

"Looks like it," said Pod.

"They may just be going the same way as us," Annalie said.

"Seriously?" said Essie.

"They're not making any moves to intercept us," Annalie said.

But they weren't moving away either. The *Sunfish* sailed on; the Admiralty vessel kept pace.

"What are they waiting for?" Will muttered. There was something so wrong about waiting to be arrested like this.

"It's Beckett, messing with us," Essie suggested.

"I'll mess with him," Will grumbled.

Every time it looked like the Admiralty were starting to veer closer, Will would steer away. After a while Annalie noticed what was happening. "I think they're trying to herd us toward the shore," she said.

They could just see a distant smudge of land on the horizon. They were definitely moving toward the coast.

"What do you think they're doing? Trying to pin us against the shore?" asked Will.

"Maybe. Or push us back into local territorial waters. Whichever it is, I know we don't want to go the way they want us to go."

"Hey, you guys," Essie interrupted. "There seems to be something going on up ahead."

The water was full of boats, none of them going anywhere in a hurry. They were mostly small- to medium-sized vessels: fishing boats, sailing boats, pleasure craft, and little working boats. Annalie looked at the flotilla through the binoculars.

"I think it's a boat race," she said. "And by the looks of things, we're just in time for the start!"

"A boat race!" Will said, and grinned. He turned the wheel.

"What are you doing?" Annalie asked.

"Best place to hide one little wooden boat is in the middle of lots of other little wooden boats," he said.

They sailed toward the crowd of spectators. Many boats had already taken up the best positions around the starting line and along the course, which was marked with colored buoys; many more were arriving late and jockeying for position. Engines blurted and surged; boats maneuvered; skippers shouted angrily at each other. Will took the *Sunfish* right into the middle of it, braving the shouts and the near misses, navigating with his engine on quarter speed.

The patrol boat was still just visible, hugging the horizon, although the other boats mostly blocked their view now.

They drew closer to the starting line. The racing boats were tacking and jostling, waiting for the starter's gun; Will looked at them enviously, admiring their elegant shapes, the huge spans of sail. They were the thoroughbreds of the sea, and he would have loved a chance to take one for a spin. Two of the yachts almost collided, and the audience shouted excitedly. Then the starter's gun blasted, and the boats were off.

Will idled, enjoying the start of the race, almost forgetting why they were there, watching as the great sails filled and the yachts maneuvered to cut each other off. Their hulls, lifted by all that magnificent canvas, barely seemed to touch the water. Soon enough the contestants had passed, along with a good proportion of the crowd who fancied testing their vessels against the kings of the sea. Will joined the followers as they danced into the wake of the race, just one among twenty or thirty little boats with nothing to do and nowhere to be on this crisp windy day in early spring, joining the loose convoy of happy, larking vessels— some fast, some not, but all out for a good time—as they sailed down the coast. They quickly lost sight of the racing yachts, and after a few hours most of the other vessels had dropped away and turned back to their home port, although there were a few, like the *Sunfish*, still sailing south.

Pod scanned the horizon through the binoculars, looking in every direction.

"See anything?" Will asked.

"Nope," Pod said. "I think we lost them."

The next destination

There were now just two scientists left on the list: Ganaman Kiveshalan (or Vesh) and Sola Prentice. According to Spinner's list, Vesh lived in a town on the border of Brundisi, while Sola had somehow managed to get all the way to Sundia. Both places were infamous, although for different reasons.

Brundisi's government had developed and used the Collodius Device. Even forty years later they were still a pariah nation, sunk in poverty, with dire water problems that the Device, ironically, had done nothing to solve.

Sundia was a huge island nation, remote and isolated in the southern ocean, south and west of the Moon Islands. It had once been a popular holiday destination for people with the time to make the long journey south; but in the troubled years leading up to the Flood, it had taken an increasingly isolationist stance. After the Flood, the Sundians had closed their borders, and they hadn't just closed their borders to refugees; they'd closed their borders to *everyone*—all ships, all nations, even the Admiralty. Ships that approached Sundia were warned, chased away, and sometimes sunk. No one could get in; no one could get out. It was a mystery how Sola Prentice had got there.

"So it seems pretty obvious we go to Brundisi next," Will said. They had sat down together around the saloon table to discuss the next leg of their journey. "I mean, I've got no idea how you'd even land in Sundia, so really there isn't much of a choice."

"Isn't Brundisi kind of dangerous?" Essie said.

"No more than the Moon Islands," Will said.

They continued on toward the south, planning the next stage of their journey. They would need to reprovision; they debated whether they should do that in one of the northern countries and risk being spotted by the authorities, or in Brundisi, where there were few authorities but lots of pirates. They decided to take a chance on the northern countries. Annalie chose a quiet town she'd visited with Spinner.

As they sailed toward the port, busy allocating tasks (Pod would fill the water tanks, Essie would get provisions), they heard a shell chime.

"We must be in range," Essie said, and jumped up and went into the cabin to fetch her shell. When she came back, she was carrying both shells.

"Annalie," she said, a strange look on her face. "You've got a message."

Annalie's heart began to beat faster as she reached for the shell. The message said: *Annalie and Will, I know you've been looking for me. I'm desperate to see you both. I'm in Gloradol and I'm safe for now but I can only stay for a week and then I'll have to move on. Please hurry. All my love, Spinner.*

Tests

All four of them gathered around the shell to read and re-read the message, which also contained an address and a map reference.

"This is it!" Will said. "It's what we've been waiting for!" He turned to Annalie. "We're obviously going, right?"

"Yes. I suppose so," Annalie said, still rather dazed by the shock of it. "After all this time, he sends a message now. So weird."

"Wait, when did he send this?" asked Will.

Essie checked the date on the message. "Two days ago."

"That means we've only got five days until he leaves again," Will said. "We've got to get to Gloradol!"

Gloradol was the old capital of Hesh, built more than five hundred years ago from land reclaimed from the sea and protected by dykes. It had been inundated and almost completely destroyed by the Flood, but the Heshans had built an enormous—an *enormous*—sea wall, pumped out the ocean, and had begun to rebuild their old city again, even more splendidly than before. Hesh was Norlind's southern neighbor; it wasn't a big country, and they had already sailed past it. The yacht race had taken a southerly route, and Will had kept them on their southerly course while they were considering where to go next. They had come a reasonable distance south; going to Gloradol would mean retracing their steps.

"Can we get there in time?" asked Essie.

"We have to," Will said.

"Now that we know he's there and contactable, we can just call him and tell him to wait," Annalie said.

Will looked at her eagerly. "All right, let's do it, let's call him now!"

They put the shell on speaker and Annalie pressed the call button, her hand trembling so much with excitement she could hardly keep the shell still. They listened to it ring, then an electronic voice said, "This shell is enabled for text only."

Will and Annalie looked at each other in confusion. "What does that mean?" Annalie asked.

"You can't call him. You can only send him a message," Essie said.

"But why?" asked Will.

Essie shrugged. "I dunno. I think it's cheaper. Or the audio might not be working."

"Maybe he can't talk," Will suggested. "Maybe he has to stay really quiet, because he's in hiding."

"Could be," Annalie said, thinking of old wartime stories about people concealed inside hidden rooms.

"Or," Pod said, "he doesn't want to talk to you because then you'd know it isn't really him."

Will looked at Pod. "What do you mean?"

201

"Doesn't it seem a bit suspicious to you?" Pod said. "After all this time, he sends you a message saying 'hurry, come and meet me here,' and he's chosen somewhere really close to the last place Beckett knows we were, and you can't even speak to him."

Essie swallowed, looking uneasily at Annalie and Will. "He does have a point."

"Well, let's just ask him then," Will said. He grabbed the shell and typed: *Why Gloradol? And how come it's taken you so long to reply to all our messages? W*

They waited for a reply. It came quickly enough: *My shell was taken from me and I've been out of range for a long time. I thought you were both safe back in Dux. I had no idea you'd come after me. Why did you do that??? Gloradol was not my choice but it's where I ended up. Does this mean you're coming? Where are you now? Are you far away?*

Will began typing again, but Pod warned, "Don't tell him."

"But what if it's him?" Will said.

"He hasn't said anything that would prove that it really is him yet," Annalie said, torn between her desire to believe and her fear that Pod might be right.

"Okay," Will said. "Let's test him." He typed: *What's my middle name?*

The answer came back: *You don't have one.*

"True," Will said.

"Who was I named after?" Annalie suggested.

The main character in your mother's favorite book.

"How did you get Graham?" Pod asked.

There was a longer pause this time before the answer came through. Will read it aloud. "'I was investigating a university science lab not long after the Flood. There were rooms full of empty cages. I found Graham in an office, sitting on top of a cabinet. The scientists had set him free when the Flood came, but he had nowhere to go, so he went back to his lab. He was very thin and very hungry. I fed him, and he stayed with me.'"

Pod turned to Graham. "*Is* that how you met Spinner?"

"Spinner had biscuit," Graham said, bobbing up and down.

"What kind of biscuit?" Pod asked. "Do you remember?"

"Anchor," Graham said promptly. "Very hard."

Anchor biscuits were Admiralty emergency rations. They were not very tasty and hard as concrete (the joke was they were made from actual anchors), but they were nutritious.

Will typed. *What did you feed Graham?*

There was another pause. Then the answer appeared. *Not sure. Probably an Anchor biscuit.*

"You see?" Will said, relieved. "It has to be him!"

"Or a lucky guess," Pod mumbled.

"He knew all the answers," Will said. "It's him! Can't you be happy about it?"

Pod's face closed. "Just want to be sure," he growled.

"So?" Will turned to Annalie, to Essie. "We're going, right?"

"He did know all the answers," Annalie said, wanting to be convinced.

Essie looked from Annalie to Will. "You're never going to be able to live with it if we don't go, are you?"

"Nope," Will said. He grabbed the shell and typed triumphantly: *We're on our way. Don't leave without us!*

The answer came promptly: *I'll be right here waiting for you.*

Gloradol

They provisioned as quickly as they could, then turned around and began to sail north with all speed. They would not sail directly into Gloradol—the great port had a naval base attached; it would be like walking into a lion's den. They agreed that the *Sunfish* would stay at sea while Will and Annalie went ashore, then made their way overland to the address Spinner had given them. Essie and Pod would stay on the boat, far enough from shore to stay out of trouble, but close enough to be within communication range.

"This could be it," Essie said as they sat around the table eating their dinner. "The end of our journey."

"It won't be the end, even if we do find him," Will said expansively, helping himself to seconds. "We'll still have Beckett on our tail, and he'll still have to work out what to do with the research. But at least we won't be chasing round the world not knowing where we're going."

"Spinner might try and send you back to school," Essie said, teasing Annalie.

"He can try," Annalie said, laughing.

"He might have some ideas about how we can get your sister back, too," Will said, trying to include Pod. Pod had been in a glum mood since they'd made the decision to go to Gloradol, and nothing could shake him out of it.

"Maybe," Pod said.

The winds were against them; it took many days to beat back to the north. There was a storm in the offing and the seas were rough and miserable. Will was almost beside himself with impatience as the original time frame came and went; Annalie had to remind him that Spinner knew they were coming, and there was no way he would leave without them.

At last they reached the place where they'd decided to go ashore. Essie hugged Annalie and then Will as they prepared to depart. "Stay in touch," she said. "Don't leave us in suspense."

"You sure about this?" Pod asked, scowling.

"We have to go," Will said. "We've got to know."

"Be careful," Pod warned.

"Always am."

"Be carefuller."

Will grinned. "Come on, Graham. Ready to go see Spinner?"

Graham let out an ear-splitting shriek. Then the three of them clambered into the dinghy and puttered away toward the distant shore, through sheeting rain that quickly hid them from view.

"It's going to be okay," Essie said, seeing Pod's bleak expression.

"Hope so," Pod said.

Hesh was a very flat country, and Will and Annalie could see the Great Sea Wall of Gloradol from a long, long way away. It was a vast construction of reinforced concrete that reared up into the sky, with a walkway cantilevered off the top, dizzyingly high, so you could walk the perimeter of the city and its wall if you chose to. Today was not a day for sightseeing: rain clouds seemed to sit just above the wall, swirling menacingly.

The closer they got to the city, the larger the wall seemed to grow. "Imagine if you lived in the shadow of that thing," Will said. "You'd never see the sunlight."

"They thought of that," Annalie said. "They've got mirrors."

She pointed out angled, mirrored panels high up above the streets that reflected sunlight into the dark spaces under the wall.

Gloradol was new to them; in all their travels with Spinner, they had never been here before. It was a slightly confounding city, for although it looked very old, it had been almost completely rebuilt. Gloradol had survived many floodings—the Flood was not its first, although it was probably the worst—and so the Heshans were old hands at picking up the pieces and putting them back just as they were. The narrow streets of Gloradol were still laid out in exactly the same way as they had been two hundred years ago, before the invention of motor vehicles, and the houses had been rebuilt in the old Gloradol style, tall and narrow, with layer on layer of distinctive curved windows, and flat roofs, some topped with gardens. The grand old manor houses, government buildings, and museums had been restored to their former glory, and the toppled cathedral had been so carefully rebuilt you would never know it was not the sixteenth-century original.

It was funny, Annalie thought, as the smooth, comfortable, and silent electric tram moved them efficiently through the streets, how different things could be from one country to the next. Everyone was hit by the same Flood, but some places were still in ruins, even now, and other places, like Gloradol, were so beautiful it was almost like the Flood had never happened. She'd seen pictures of the ruins of Gloradol—it made for a memorable history lesson—but to look at the city now, so comfortable and prosperous and elegant, it was hard to believe it was the same place. The only reminder of what had happened was the wall, which was hard to miss, since it was taller than almost every other building in this low-rise metropolis, and if you were facing in the right direction you couldn't help but see it, looming over everything.

They watched the streets go by, gray and glistening, as rain began to patter tentatively at the windows.

"Where do you suppose the rainwater goes when your city's built below sea level?" she said.

Will blinked, suddenly recognizing the problem.

"I don't know," he said. "But it has to go somewhere, or that wall's going to turn this city into a dam."

"I'm going to find out," Annalie said.

She searched the links, looking for answers. "They have a state of the art system that kicks in whenever the water levels get too high," she reported. "The stormwater gets channelled into canals and then they pump it through the wall and into the sea."

"Huh," Will said, only momentarily interested by the engineering problem. His mind was on other things. "Do you think he's going to be mad at us for coming after him?"

Annalie knew he was talking about Spinner. "I don't know," she said. "Probably."

"We had good reasons for coming," Will said.

"I know."

"And at least we made it here in one piece. That's something, right?"

"Definitely."

They thought about this for a bit. "I think he'll still be mad," Annalie said finally. "Happy, but mad. This is our stop."

Before Will and Annalie left the *Sunfish*, they'd spent a lot of time planning the best way to approach the place where Spinner was holed up. Essie had gone to work on her shell, pulling up pictures of the district, the streets, the building itself. They'd studied these carefully, working out the best ways in and out, possible escape routes, danger points, and hazards. They wanted to be sure that once they were reunited with Spinner, they knew the quickest way to get out of there and back to the boat. "Because every time we go on land," Will said, "something seems to go wrong."

They alighted from the tram, Graham riding on Will's shoulder. It made them a little conspicuous, but Graham had refused to be carried. He was still, perhaps, traumatized by the Norlind police and their cardboard box. They were on a pleasant avenue lined with trees that were just coming into spring bud. Spinner was staying in an apartment building not far from the tram stop.

"See if you can get him to come to you," Pod had suggested.

"Why?" asked Will.

"Because then you can make sure it's really him before you let him see you," Pod said.

There was a large park not far from the apartment building, and they'd chosen this as a possible meeting place. The rain started whispering down again as Will and Annalie walked to the park.

"Let's find somewhere to wait out of the rain," Will said.

They found a tree; it didn't offer much shelter, but it was better than nothing. Will scanned the park, which was deserted apart from one or two hurrying pedestrians, while Annalie sent a message: *We're here. Come to the park at the end of the street. We'll meet you at the fountain.*

There was a pause. Then the answer came back: *I'm afraid I can't do that. You'll need to come here.*

Why? Annalie typed.

I was injured and I'm not very mobile. I didn't tell you before because I didn't want to worry you—it's not very serious. But you'll have to come to me. I'm really looking forward to seeing you both.

Annalie looked at Will, worried. "I wonder how bad it is," she said. "What if we can't get him back to the *Sunfish*?"

"We'll work it out when we see him," Will said. "Let's just find him."

He could hardly stand still, he was so eager to be off.

"Are you sure about this?" Annalie asked.

"We've come this far," Will said. "He's injured. He needs us."

Annalie was suddenly overtaken by the memory of Essie in her orange life jacket being dragged away from her by the storm. She remembered the terror in Essie's face, the look of utter helplessness and despair as she saw her friend failing to help her, and all Pod's warnings melted away. They'd come all this way to find Spinner. They had to go and get him.

"Okay," she said.

The building was four storeys high, with one apartment per floor; Spinner was on the top floor. Each apartment number had a buzzer beside it.

"Here goes," said Will, and pressed the buzzer.

They waited, breathless. The door clicked open, but no one spoke through the intercom. Will pushed

211

open the door and they went inside.

The building was quiet. It was the middle of the day; perhaps all the occupants were at work.

Will and Annalie climbed the stairs cautiously, Graham flying ahead of them. The stairwell was unlit, but fingers of light crept through small windows on the landings.

They reached the fourth floor and stopped, although the stairs continued, leading to the roof. The door to apartment four was closed.

Annalie and Will exchanged a shivery, excited glance, then Annalie raised her hand and knocked.

The door swung open, and a familiar shape loomed in the doorway. But it was not the familiar shape they'd been hoping to see.

"Hello, Annalie. Will. Nice to see you again." Beckett gave them a toothy smile.

They heard footsteps behind them and turned to see a marine coming down the stairs that led to the roof, while another came into view in the staircase just below them, cutting off both escape routes.

They were trapped.

The Trans-Northern Express

"Someone catch that bird!" Beckett ordered, but Graham was too quick for them. He shot off down the stairwell, shrieking in rage. Annalie watched him go, hoping he'd get out of there safely.

"You'd better come in," Beckett said.

He stood aside and let them walk into the apartment. It was simple and empty, barely furnished. From the entranceway, they walked into a single room with a little kitchen off to one side and large windows at the end that looked out onto sheeting gray rain. Other doors led, presumably, to bedrooms and the bathroom, although these were all closed.

One of the marines followed Beckett into the room and stood guard at the front door to prevent an escape.

"Is he here?" Will asked aggressively.

"Of course not," Beckett said. "Did you really believe he was?" He gave Will a pitying look. "You poor children."

This made Will's blood boil, as it was meant to. "You're never going to find him," he said. "Even if you catch us, you'll never get what you're really looking for."

"*If* I catch you?" Beckett said. "I *have* caught you." He smiled unpleasantly. "So I take it you haven't heard from your father in a while?"

"Yes, we have," Will said.

"Really?" Beckett smiled. "He's had an interesting journey, hasn't he?"

"Let's cut the chitchat," Will said. "We're not going to tell you where he is, okay?"

"You don't have to," Beckett said. "I already know where he is. I caught him, on the Trans-Northern Express. And I'm afraid I have some bad news for you." He paused, a master showman. "Your father is dead."

Annalie felt the shock of this like a physical blow. The breath went out of her.

"You're lying!" Will shouted.

"I'm afraid I'm not," Beckett said. "I was looking forward to bringing him to trial and throwing the book at him so I could sentence him to rot in a jail of my choosing for the rest of his days, or maybe, if I got the right judge, have him sentenced to death for treason. We still have the death penalty for treason, you know. But when we came to arrest him, he tried to jump off the train. Did you know the Trans-Northern Express travels at one hundred and twenty-five miles an hour? No one can survive a fall like that—not even Spinner. So, disappointing for all of us, but especially disappointing for you."

Beckett waited to see what they'd do.

Will flew at him, punching and hitting him, swearing and shouting.

Beckett fended him off with ease. "It really was an accident, if it makes you feel any better. I would much rather have brought him in for questioning, but obviously that's impossible now."

Annalie felt dizzy. Could it be true? She tried to cling onto the knowledge that Spinner had been alive and well in Norlind not long ago; but she had no way of knowing what had happened after that. If it really was true, and they were actually alone in the world... Her mind turned away from the terrible thought.

But then she considered Beckett's watchful eyes, his disdainful amusement, and she felt a tiny finger of doubt. He had tricked them into coming here. What if this was just one more trick? Could he be lying?

She grabbed onto this thought and did her best to banish the fear and grief that was threatening to shut down her brain. She was going to need all her wits about her if they had any hope of getting out of this.

"If Spinner's already dead, why are you still chasing us?" she challenged. "You know we can't lead you to him now."

Beckett turned to her, a glitter of dislike in his eyes. "He died before he could give me what I'm looking for," he said. "The location of the research."

"We don't know where it is," Annalie said.

"You're lying," he said. "I *know* you're lying. I was on Little Lang Lang. Art told me what he saw. You've got the research, and I want it."

"We don't have it anymore," Will said. "We lost it."

Beckett turned to him. "Honestly, Will," he said.

"How stupid do you think I am?"

"There was a storm," Will said stubbornly. "A lot of stuff went overboard; we nearly sank. We were lucky to escape with our lives. We don't have it anymore."

Beckett gave him a dead-eyed smile. "Enough. I'm taking you into custody." He signaled to the marine at the door.

"Wait!" Will said. "I need to use the bathroom."

Beckett narrowed his eyes, weighing this up, then said, "Fine." He pointed to one of the doors, and Will disappeared through it.

"Where will you take us?" Annalie asked, partly because she wanted to know and partly because she thought she should keep Beckett talking.

"We'll take you two and your little friend back to Dux. As for your boat, we'll strip it down to the nails and timbers."

"You can't do that!" Annalie protested. "It's the only thing we've got left! Where we will go? Where will we live?"

"That's not really my problem, is it?" Beckett said. His head turned toward the bathroom, as if wondering how long Will was going to be.

Seeing this, Annalie said, "But please, it's the only thing of Spinner's we've got left. Isn't there something we can do so you don't have to destroy the boat?"

"Of course there is," Beckett said impatiently. "Tell me where the research is."

"Will's telling the truth! We don't know where it is!" Annalie cried.

"Then we're at an impasse, aren't we?" Beckett went to the bathroom door and gave a knock. "Will? Taking your time in there, aren't you?"

A muffled voice said, "Just a minute!"

From the corner of her eye, Annalie caught a flash of movement. She looked over at the long window at the end of the room and saw a blaze of feathers: *Graham!* He was hovering beside the window, looking in at her. As soon as he saw her looking his way, he flew to one side of the window and hovered there with an expectant look. He performed the same action again, and then spiraled up out of sight. Annalie knew he'd been trying to signal something, but could not work out what it was. What was he trying to tell her?

"Will?" Beckett said again. "Open this door."

This time there was no answer. Beckett tried the door, his face darkening with rage, but of course it was locked.

"Break this door down!" he ordered.

The marine left his post by the front door and began to shoulder-charge the bathroom door.

Annalie saw Graham appear at the window again. He flicked his wing tips upward, circled around, and then disappeared upward once again. This time she guessed his meaning: the roof. Graham was heading for the roof. Did that mean Will was too? She felt a quiver of fear at the thought of Will shinning up a drainpipe four storeys in the air.

The lock on the bathroom door gave and the door crashed open.

Annalie seized the moment. While Beckett

and the marine were focused on the bathroom, she ran for the front door and slipped out. Behind her Beckett roared with rage; Will had escaped. A second marine was stationed at the top of the stairs that led down; he shouted as he saw Annalie emerge, but he was just far enough away that she was able to get past him and race up the stairs to the roof. She slammed the door behind her, but there was no lock on the outside; she was going to have to wedge it shut. She looked around frantically, hoping to see something, anything, she could stick under the door handle.

"Here!" Will shouted, running toward her holding a deckchair with a rotted canvas cover. Together they wedged it under the door handle.

"Bathroom window, huh?" Annalie said.

"Did you see how small it was?" Will said. "What about you?"

"Went out the front door while they were looking for you."

"Nice. Let's go."

They started to run. The building was part of a terraced row, and the roofs had a gentle slope to let the rain run off. The rain had grown heavier while they were inside the building; it was thundering down now in a dense wall of water, and the roofs were ankle-deep, so they had to be careful how they placed their feet.

Behind them they could hear determined crashing and bashing as the marines attempted to break down the door. They hurtled through flapping sheets and vaulted over planter boxes, past an aviary filled with cooing pigeons. Once, Will put his foot right through the roof.

There was a distant crash behind them and they heard shouts. Will glanced back. "They've got the door open," he panted. "They're coming."

They had a good headstart, but they had shorter legs than the marines.

"No more roof!" Graham squawked from above.

They had come to the end of the row. Empty air was on three sides of them and it was four storeys down to the street.

Will rushed to the closest roof door and tried it. It was locked.

"Now what?" asked Annalie.

They looked around them. They could move back along the row, trying the doors until they found one that opened, but with every second that passed, the marines were getting closer. Running back toward them didn't seem like a good idea.

"Tree!" Graham squawked.

Will spun around to see what Graham was talking about.

Behind the last house, a tall tree lifted its branches into the air. Graham swirled about and landed in the uppermost branches. "Here!" he squawked.

"You're a bird," Annalie shouted. "We're not!"

Will was measuring the distance with his eye, considering the thickness of the canopy. "I reckon we could make that," he said. "It might hurt a bit. But if you jump out and grab onto something, we could get down that tree."

"I'm not jumping into that!" Annalie said. It was way too far. She wasn't especially bothered by heights, but the gap was large, and she wasn't sure that she had the strength to catch herself as she fell into the canopy and prevent herself from dropping the four storeys to the ground.

"Fine. Stay and get caught then," Will said. And without another thought, he backed up, took a run up, and leaped.

Out he went, out into the terrible empty air, his arms windmilling as he propelled himself forward through the rain. He crashed into the upper branches, grabbing and slipping, and fell, fell, fell—until he hit a larger branch with an audible *oof*, and managed to grab on. He looked up, winded but triumphant, to see Annalie looking down at him. "Come on!" he yelled.

The marines were only two rooftops away. They were shouting at her as they advanced, demanding she surrender.

She followed Will's lead. She jumped.

Branches thrashed at her, she fell and slipped and was cut in a thousand places by the whippy twigs. Time seemed to slow in the terror of falling. She glanced off a biggish branch, slick and wet, then bounced onto another, reaching desperately for something that would slow her fall. She grabbed an armful of branch and caught it, dangling in the air like a kitten. She kicked wildly with her legs—her toe found something—and at last she had a branch to stand on.

Will was already scrambling down as quickly as he could. "Come on! They're probably circling round to cut us off already!" he said.

The two of them climbed down the tree, Graham flitting from branch to branch.

"Graham," Will said, "go and work out where the marines are."

Graham flew off as they landed on solid ground. Will's eyes darted around, looking for the next escape route. *Through the building? Over the wall into the next garden?* They waited, hiding behind the tree, as Graham flew a loop, scouting the streets.

"Go this way. Next street," he said, perching on the garden's back wall. Another row of terraces lay back-to-back with this one. Will and Annalie struggled over the high stone wall and landed cautiously in the next yard, not knowing what they might find. The sheeting rain meant visibility was poor, which was both an advantage and a disadvantage. The yard was empty, but the door into the building was locked.

"Next one," Will said.

They helped each other over the wall into the next yard, where a dog snoozed. It woke as they landed and began barking violently.

"Not here, either," Will said. They ran across the yard and flew over the fence. The next yard was dog-free and quiet; even better, the back door was unlocked. Will and Annalie hurried along the hallway, and then peeped out the glass front door.

"See anything?" Annalie asked.

"Nope," Will said.

He opened the door and peered around it, looking for marines. He couldn't see any.

"Okay, let's go," he said.

They stepped out the door, crossed the road, and ran up the street, trying to put some distance between themselves and the marines. The streets were a river. There was so much water pouring out of the sky that it was coming down faster than the gutters could drain it away.

"There they are!"

Two marines were running toward them.

"Come on!" Will said.

They changed direction and ran on, splashing through the cascade that was pouring down the footpath. Behind them, the marines were calling for back-up. Already tired, Annalie knew she could not stay ahead of a team of marines for long.

"I don't know how long I can keep this up," she gasped to Will.

"Try!" Will panted back.

They ran for their lives, dodging down street after street, trying everything they could to evade the marines. But the marines kept coming.

They turned and ducked and dived, with no idea of where they were going in the unfamiliar terrain of this orderly city. The rain thrummed down on them, and Graham soared ahead, scouting. They turned down a street, which looked open at the other end. Graham came looping back to them.

"No good!" he shrieked. "River!"

The marines were in the street behind them now, blocking their escape. They had no choice but to keep going forward, toward the river.

"That's not a river," Annalie panted, as they got closer to it. "That's a canal."

They reached the end of the street. Another street crossed it, running parallel to the canal, and as they turned left to go down it, they saw, to their horror, a second team of marines coming toward them. They turned back to go the other way down the cross street. A third team was coming from that direction. They were trapped.

"Come on, kids," one of the marines called. "There's nowhere for you to go. It's time to stop running."

"Never!" Will shouted.

The marines had dropped to a walk now, advancing toward them steadily, confident they had them cornered.

"We just want to talk to you," the marine said. "There's no need for all this running around."

"You know," Will muttered, "he's so right."

Without giving her even the slightest warning, he grabbed Annalie, rushed her to the edge of the canal, and launched them both in.

Downstream

The current was faster and more powerful than Will had expected. The marines chased after them for a while, but then the canal moved away from the road and was enclosed by fences, making pursuit impossible, and Will savored the marines' furious expressions as the water bore them away.

"So long, suckers!" he crowed.

Annalie was coughing and spluttering—she'd swallowed water when she fell in. "What is wrong with you?" she gasped.

"We got away, didn't we?" Will said.

Conversation was difficult over the roar of the water. The canal was deeper than it looked; Will's feet touched nothing as they were borne along, and when he tried to reach for the bottom, he simply sank.

"How are we going to get out of here?" Annalie said.

"Put some distance between us and them first," Will said.

The water tumbled them along. It was not nice water: brown and swirling, it was filled with rubbish, it smelled, and it was freezing cold. Unseen objects below the surface bumped against them. The sides of the canals were sloping concrete, smooth and unobstructed, built to transfer water fast. He could already tell it would be difficult to get out of these canals unless you could find something hanging down to grab onto.

The rain was still thumping down. The water level was almost visibly rising, and the current was pulling him ahead of Annalie. He didn't want to risk losing her. He struggled to swim against the tide, reaching out to grab onto her. "We need to stay together," he said. "If you see anything that floats, grab it."

Annalie's teeth were chattering. "Got to get out of this water," she said.

Looking ahead, he saw a tree branch hanging down. "Look!" he said, pointing.

As they swept under the branch, Will reached for it and managed to grab hold. Annalie reached up too, but missed. Will struggled to hold onto the branch with one hand, Annalie with the other, but the current was dragging her away from him, and it was more powerful than he was. His fingers lost their grip on the branch. They were carried away once more.

"Sorry," she gasped.

"We'll get the next one," he said.

But another one didn't come. The water swept them on and on, while Graham flew above them, shrieking in distress. Something heavy struck Will in the leg, shocking him with the pain. He began to be afraid of catching on underwater obstacles, getting pinned and trapped, drowning.

"Oh no!" Annalie squeaked. "Tunnel!"

Ahead of them, the open canal became an enclosed culvert. There was no time to imagine what they might be headed toward. In moments, they were racing into the darkness. Will took an enormous breath as the blackness closed around him. He remembered what Annalie had said about the stormwater system in Gloradol: they pumped the water out to sea. He felt cold and terrified as he imagined pumps and turbines and long dark tunnels. Could they have any hope of surviving being pumped through a stormwater system?

Just as suddenly, they were out in the daylight again. The tunnel had been simply a bridge or a structural reinforcement, and now they were out in the open canal once more. But the thought of the pumping station had made Will nervous. Looking up, he saw that the wall was getting closer—a lot closer.

"We've got to get out of this water before we hit the wall," he said.

They scanned the bank anxiously for anything that might give them a handhold. The water was moving very fast, and the wall drew closer and closer and closer, looming even more threateningly now than it had before.

"There!" Annalie shouted.

A metal bridge spanned the canal, an intricate lacework of steel. It was a narrow bridge, built for pedestrians, not vehicles. It was built well above the top of the concrete walls of the canal, and Will wasn't sure he could even reach it, let alone grab onto it and pull himself up. But he knew they would have to try.

The water swept them toward the bridge. Will counted them in: "One, two, three!"

They both kicked up and grabbed. Will's fingers slammed painfully into the metal, but he managed to get a hand on it, and held on with all his might. He saw Annalie miss the first jump, try again, and just manage to get a grip on the other side before she was swept away. Will got both hands onto the metal underside of the bridge, the current dragging at his legs, and tried to pull himself up, but couldn't. He hung there, feeling the strain, knowing his grip wouldn't last much longer, but then saw Annalie on the other side of the bridge kick up with her legs, hook her feet into the structure, and scramble monkey-like, using hands and feet, over the side and onto the clanging metal walkway. Following her lead, he swung his legs up, found a toehold of his own, and scrambled painfully and laboriously up.

"Look," Annalie said when he'd slumped down, exhausted, onto the walkway.

Just downstream, the canal fed into a huge collection pond. At the far end of the pond, machinery on an industrial scale loomed; the roar of the water reached a crescendo there. On the far side of the pond, behind the machinery, rose the wall. Will noticed a piece of colorful junk borne swiftly along by the current. It floated out into the middle of the pond, drifted in an arc, but was then drawn inexorably toward the machinery at the far end, where the water became turbid. The piece of junk swirled once frantically, then was sucked under and disappeared, never to rise again.

"You think that's it?" he asked.

Annalie nodded.

Will felt a shiver pass over him. "That was close," he said.

"Yep," Annalie said.

Neither of them said anything for a while.

The rain continued, making progress unpleasant, but it had the advantage of partially hiding them from view. Almost no one was out on the streets in this tempest. They knew the marines were probably still on the lookout for them, so they wasted no time getting away from the canals.

Annalie's shell did not work after its immersion, so they could not send a message or even check their location, but it was not hard to work out where they needed to go: all they had to do was follow the wall until they were out of the city. This took some time; the wall was vast. But they made it back to the dinghy without any further entanglements, and soon they were puttering through the driving rain to where the *Sunfish* lay at anchor, waiting for them.

Pod looked down at them over the side, swathed in Spinner's wet weather gear. "Well?" he asked.

Will shook his head.

Pod helped them both aboard without another word.

After Gloradol

"Do you think he was telling the truth?" Essie asked. "Is Spinner really dead?"

Will and Annalie looked at each other.

"How can you tell with a guy like that?" Will said.

"He could've been telling the truth," Annalie said. "But I have a feeling he was lying."

"He *must* have been lying," Will decided.

"Something tells me he hasn't laid a finger on Spinner yet, even after Sujana betrayed him, and that's why he keeps coming after us," Annalie said. "It's because he hasn't got a clue where Spinner is."

Will's face brightened a little. "Maybe we're all he's got."

"Exactly," Annalie said. "Which is why we've got to stay ahead of him now."

Will turned to look at her. "So where are we going?"

"It has to be Brundisi, right?"

The sailing route was a long one: back down the coast of the north lands, around the great horn of Estilo, through the Bostoroso Strait, and then east, until they reached Brundisi. The Sea of Brundisi was known for its horrible storms, and also for pirates. Brundisi and its neighbors were some of the poorest nations in the world; piracy was the only industry that thrived.

The journey took them several weeks, and their supplies began to run down. After they passed the Bostoroso Strait, they decided to put in for supplies at one of the last ports in Estilo. After Estilo, things rapidly got a lot less safe.

As they drew in to port, Essie's shell, as ever, began chiming merrily—and this time it was full of surprises.

"Guess what?" she said, looking up from her messages. "I've been kidnapped!"

The kidnapping of Essie

TOWER CORP HEIRESS KIDNAPPED

Essie Wan, 13, the only daughter of disgraced Tower
Corp founder Everest Wan, has been kidnapped. It is
believed the kidnapping was masterminded by a shady
underworld figure, Ned "Spinner" Wallace, whose
daughter, Annalie Wallace (also known as Annalie
Go) was a fellow pupil at Triumph College, Pallas.
Essie Wan went missing from Triumph College over
four months ago, when she was taken from her school
dormitory by Annalie Wallace in the middle of the
night. The two girls were traced to Southaven, where
Essie was forced to access Everest Wan's creditstream
and take out a large amount of cash. Annalie and her
brother William Wallace hid Miss Wan aboard the
family vessel, the *Sunfish*, which then escaped into
international waters. Investigators believe Miss Wan
is still being held captive aboard the *Sunfish*, and they
are making vigorous efforts to trace the vessel.

The fugitives have continued to access Everest
Wan's creditstream, stealing substantial amounts of
money before it was closed down. Events took a new

turn on Monday when, for the first time in this long-running case, a ransom demand was received. The full details of the demand have not been revealed, but it has been reported that the kidnappers are asking for a substantial sum of money to guarantee Miss Wan's safe return.

Through his lawyers, Everest Wan begged for the safe return of his daughter. "She is the most precious thing in all the world to me, and she is dearly and profoundly loved and missed. Please return her safely to the people who care about her the most." A spokesman for Mr. Wan reported that they were pursuing all avenues to ensure his daughter's safe return.

The timing of the kidnapping demand is puzzling. Everest Wan, formerly one of Dux's wealthiest property developers, has had his bank accounts frozen by prosecutors until the case against him can be heard, which would make it difficult for him to access the large sums of money required to pay a ransom demand.

Essie Wan's mother, who is separated from Everest Wan, and is reportedly engaged to billionaire shipping magnate Linkon Vanafatsulu, made this comment on her personal news stream: "Hoping and praying my baby girl comes back to me soon safe & sound." Her fiancé has declined to comment on the matter, saying through a spokesperson: "My wife and I ask for privacy at this difficult and distressing time." The spokesperson would not comment on whether Mr. Vanafatsulu might be willing to pay the ransom.

A description of the boat and the kidnappers has been issued to police forces and marine authorities worldwide. They have been warned to be on the alert for these dangerous criminals.

"I wish they'd said how much the ransom is," Essie said, laughing. "I want to know how much I'm worth."

Annalie didn't think there was anything funny about the story. "But what is this even about? What ransom? What's going on?"

"It's obviously a joke," Essie said.

"It's no joke," Annalie said. "It's made us a target. Do you think your parents have done this, to get you back?"

"They want me to come home," Essie said, "but why make up all that stuff about a ransom? It's just weird."

"I know who did this," Will said suddenly. "Beckett. When he caught me back in the Moon Islands, he threatened to have us charged with kidnapping. Looks like he's gone and done it."

"Why wait all this time?" asked Annalie.

"Because he's running out of options," Will said. "He keeps trying to catch us and we keep getting away. It can't look too good to his superiors. He's trying to put the pressure on us. Now we're not just fugitives. We're kidnappers. Everyone's going to be looking for us. Not just harbormasters, *everybody*. And now they know what we look like."

The article was lavishly illustrated, with an adorable picture of Essie, shots of Will and Annalie looking subtly unpleasant (they appeared to have been pulled from surveillance footage and enhanced), a very out-of-date photo of Spinner, and a shot of the now-white *Sunfish*, which must have been taken when it was impounded by the Norlindens.

"What do we do?" Essie asked. "Can we risk going to shore and getting supplies? What if somebody recognizes us?"

"They don't know me," Pod said. "I'll take the dinghy."

"What about water?" Annalie said. The main tanks were built into the hull; the easiest way to fill them was to dock and take on water directly.

"We're not out of water yet," Essie said. "And we can always treat seawater if we have to."

Annalie looked dubious. She knew they'd struggle to produce enough water for the four of them plus Graham.

"We'll look for creeks and streams along the way," Will said. "Do it the old-fashioned way."

Annalie nodded. "Okay. Let's not stick around here any longer than we have to. Pod, get us some supplies."

They stood on deck as Pod went zooming off in the dinghy to buy food.

"Hey—that thing about your dad's creditstream," Will said. "The article said they'd closed it down. That's not true, is it?"

Essie looked worried. She flicked open her shell and made some clicks. Her breath caught. "Yep," she said.

"He's cut you off?" Annalie said.

"I'll tell him to switch it back on," Essie said, flicking between programs. "I'll tell him it's all a lie."

She started typing furiously, but Will stopped her. "Wait," he said, "what if that's what they want us to do?"

"What?"

"They're probably monitoring all his communications. If you write to him now and ask him to switch the money back on, they'll know. They might even be able to work out where you sent the message from."

Essie sighed. "Yes, they probably can."

"How much money do we have?" Annalie asked.

"I wouldn't say we've got tons," Essie said. "But we're okay, for now at least."

"Then we need to lie low," Will said. "Don't give them any clues. Don't send him any messages."

"But what if he thinks it's true?" Essie said, getting upset. "What if he thinks I've been kidnapped and you're going to kill me? He'll be going out of his mind with worry."

"I'd rather let him worry than let Beckett know where we are," Will said.

Essie put her head in her hands. "Why won't that guy leave us alone?" she wailed, frustrated.

Annalie patted her back and said nothing, but the look she gave Will was troubled.

Pod soon returned, the dinghy riding low in the water with the weight of all the supplies. He'd bought what they needed and more, so they wouldn't be forced ashore again in a hurry. They set a course out to sea.

Water was their next immediate concern as they resumed their journey. They took care to conserve the water they had, and Will rigged up a system that Spinner had devised to catch and channel rainwater. It was cumbersome and took up room on deck, so they didn't usually use it, but now it seemed like a good idea.

Annalie studied the charts closely, looking for

potential water sources onshore. The first two creeks they checked out were obviously unfit to drink, but the third was perfect. A thin stream of clear, cold water, swelled by spring rain, cascaded down a cliff and into the sea below. It flowed through a forest, not a town or through farmland, so they hoped it would be relatively unpolluted (although they would still filter and boil it before they drank it). They filled all the spare tanks they carried, and hoped that they might now get all the way to their destination without having to stop again.

The stop for water had, of course, taken them in close to shore. Although the creek was in a wild place, far from any towns, as they began to sail away from it, something surprising happened. They got just a wisp of signal; Essie's shell chimed; and so, once again, did Annalie's.

Annalie snatched her shell up. There was a single voice message, from an unknown source. Annalie looked at it, feeling a shiver of dread.

"Do you recognize the ID?" Essie asked, looking over her shoulder.

Annalie shook her head. "What if it's Beckett?"

"Messaging you to gloat?"

"Or threaten us."

Essie and Annalie looked at each other.

"Better listen to it," Essie said.

Annalie pressed play, expecting the worst. But the voice she heard was not Beckett's.

"Annalie! What's all this about you kidnapping some girl from college? Call me back on this number as soon as you get this!"

It was Spinner.

The real Spinner

Annalie tried immediately to call him back, but the wisp of signal had vanished. She ran up on deck, shouting excitedly to Will and Pod. "He's here, he's here, he called me! We've got to get somewhere we can link, now!"

Will made her play the message over and over again. "Why doesn't he say where he is?" he said, frustrated and thrilled in equal measure.

"We've just got to call him back!" Annalie said. "But first we need to get somewhere with signal!"

"Get the charts."

Annalie rushed to look at the charts. They were sailing past barren country, sparsely populated, but they soon located a town that seemed a likely spot. They made for it with all speed, Essie and Annalie holding their shells up the whole way.

The town drew close; shells vibrated and pinged; they were in range.

"Do you want some privacy?" Essie asked shyly.

"We're all a part of this," Annalie said. "You guys should be here too."

The four of them and Graham sat around the

table in the saloon. Will and Annalie looked at each other. "Okay," Will said. "Shall we do this?"

Annalie nodded tremulously.

They pressed the call button. The shell rang—and rang—and rang—and then it was answered.

"Annalie?" It was Spinner's voice, real and true and big as life, just as they remembered it.

"Yes, it's me," she said.

"And me!" Will said.

Graham *skrarked* hugely to show he was there too.

"All three of you!" Spinner laughed. "How are you doing, old man?"

"Spinner go away," Graham said accusingly. "Bad Spinner. No biscuit."

"I'm sorry about that," Spinner said. "None of this has really gone to plan."

"Where are you?" Annalie asked.

"And where have you been?" Will added. "Didn't you get any of our messages?"

"If I'd gotten them I would've answered them," Spinner said, surprised. "So no, I didn't get your messages. Where are *you*? And what's all this nonsense about a kidnapping?"

"They didn't kidnap me," Essie spoke up. "I came voluntarily."

"This is Essie," Annalie explained. "She's my best friend."

"I remember your friend," Spinner said slowly. Annalie had spoken about her often in her weekly calls home from school. "But I was hoping the rest of it was just an invention."

"It is," Annalie said.

"So you didn't steal money and sail off in the *Sunfish*?"

"It wasn't exactly stealing," Annalie said.

"My dad gave me that creditstream to use," Essie said, "and I used it. We needed the money."

There was a long, unsettling pause from Spinner. "Where are you now?" he asked again.

"Off Estilo," Annalie said, "in the Sea of Brundisi."

"Oh, kids," Spinner groaned. "What have you done?"

"We came to look for you," Will said.

"We found the clues you left for us," Annalie said. "We worked out you were going to find your old colleagues. We already saw Dan Gari. We ran into trouble in the Moon Islands, so we didn't get to Dasto Puri until after you'd already left. We went to try and find you at Sujana's house, but you'd already left. Spinner, I have to tell you, Sujana sold you out. After you left, she called up Beckett and told him where to find you."

"I know," Spinner said. "He almost got me too." But he didn't want to talk about Sujana. "I thought I told you to stay home and stay safe."

"But we weren't safe," Annalie said. "Beckett came to see me at Triumph. He knew about us from the start. We had to get away from him."

"They would've burned the boat too," Will said. "So I had to get it back from them. They wrecked the workshop, though."

Spinner let out a long breath. "I'm sorry," he said

finally, his voice unsteady. "I thought at least you two would be safe from him."

"It's okay," Annalie said. "We've made it this far. And at least now we know you're not dead."

"No," he said. "Not yet. Although it looked a bit dicey there a couple of times."

"Tell us about it," Will muttered.

"You still haven't told us where you are," Annalie said.

"In Brundisi," Spinner said. "With Vesh."

"So, what happened?" Will asked. "Where have you been all this time?"

Spinner's story

"The night Beckett's men came for me, I didn't have a lot of time," Spinner explained. "I had an exit strategy in place—several strategies actually—but Plan A turned out to be impossible."

"Getting away on the *Sunfish*?" Will guessed.

"Right," Spinner said. "When I got there, they already had a marine guarding the boat. So I had to look for another way out."

"So you went to the Crown and Anchor with Truman," Annalie said.

"Right again," Spinner said. "You two did some sleuthing, didn't you? I had a contact among the Kangs, and I arranged to meet him at the Crown. I knew I had to get out that night. I was lucky—they had a boat that was about to do the run to Dasto Puri, so they smuggled me aboard along with all the other illegal stuff, then I waited in the cargo hold for two more days before they actually sailed. Have you ever tried living in a cargo hold? It's not nice."

Pod was nodding. He knew all about living in a cargo hold.

"I'd made a deal with my contact that I'd pay them

some of the money upfront, and the rest would be held in a trust account by a third party and only paid out when they got me where I wanted to go. It's a pretty standard arrangement, whether you're moving illegal cigarettes or illegal people and, stupidly, I thought I could trust them because I knew the guy onshore. But he didn't come with us on the journey, he just brokered the deal, and once we got deep into the Moon Islands, someone in the crew decided to see how much more they could squeeze me for. They stopped in the middle of the ocean and threatened to toss me overboard if I didn't double the sum I'd agreed on."

"What did you do?" Will asked.

"Well, I negotiated. I said I didn't have double the sum, I only had what I'd promised because I'd had to escape at such short notice, blah, blah, blah. Eventually I managed to more or less convince them I didn't have any more money and if they threw me in the sea they really would get nothing. The captain shut it down, but I knew it hadn't really gone away. Some of the crew were looking at me funny and lurking around at night, and I just had a bad feeling somebody might try something.

"So I decided to take matters into my own hands. After we left Dux, I'd been free to move about the ship, and I'd made sure to take a good look at all the tech they had on board. You know, some of those Kang boats really are impressive. This one had the same propulsion system that some of the Admiralty boats use—"

"The wave-powered ones?" Will said eagerly.

"That's it," Spinner said. "It's a bit bolted-on, since

it's stolen, but they've got it. The boat was amazingly fast. But that's highly sophisticated technology, and if it goes wrong, you need specialist help. You can't just stick it back together with a spanner.

"So one night, something goes wrong with the wave-propulsion system, and the boat grinds to a halt."

"Something?" Will prompted.

"I *might* have had something to do with it," Spinner said. "Next day, the whole crew's going over the boat trying to work out what's gone wrong and why they're dead in the water. Eventually they realize it's the propulsion system, but there's no one on board who can fix it. They can send for help from the nearest Kang technician, but it turns out he's on Dasto Puri—days or even weeks away—and we're stuck there, a sitting duck, with a big load of cargo on board that no one wants to get caught with.

"So I said, 'I know something about wave-propulsion systems. I could take a look at it for you. But there's a price.' And the captain said, 'What price?' I said, 'You guarantee me safe passage to Dasto Puri. No little accidents, no more shakedowns, and when we do get there, I want a fifty percent discount on the fare as payment for my services. That's my price, take it or leave it. If it's too high, we can all just sit here and wait for your technician to get here, and hope no one else stumbles upon us first.'

"Well, the captain didn't want to be stuck there any longer than he had to, so he agreed to my terms and let me fix the propulsion system. I made it look like a super-complicated job: I had pirates fetching me a million different kinds of tools and gadgets and running all kinds of diagnostics. Then, when nobody was looking, I switched back the relays I'd swapped over the night before, and the whole thing started up again. I'd saved the day!"

Will and Annalie cheered.

"So we got to Dasto Puri without any further mishaps, and I met up with Dan Gari."

"Danny Boy!" said Graham.

"That's him," Spinner said. "Personally I don't know how he can live with pirates full-time. He claims they protect him, but it seems an awfully high price to pay. I wouldn't have said he seemed happy there, but there was no shifting him."

"He seemed kind of paranoid," Annalie said.

"He is paranoid," Spinner said. "Always was. Although maybe if you're working for a criminal enterprise, maybe it's not paranoid to think everyone's out to get you, since everybody is. Anyway, I'd been hoping I could stay with Dan for a while and consider my options, but he didn't want anything to do with me. The Kangs back in Dux were reporting that Beckett's lot had turned Lowtown upside down looking for me and they were scared someone might talk. So they wanted me gone as soon as possible. By that stage I was ready to say good-bye to the Kangs, and I was hoping to get to an island with a ferry service—or anything, really—but you know how it is on Puri. They control who comes onto the island and who goes off it, and the only way off was on another one of their boats. So, reluctantly, I paid them again and left Puri with a different bunch of Kangs.

"It was a smaller boat this time. Not as fast. I don't know what their mission was. I was going to hop off at the first land we came to, but I didn't get the chance. We were caught in a shocker of a storm and the boat started taking on water. The crew started fighting about what to do—stay with the boat and try to save it, or abandon ship. If it'd been up to me, I would've stayed with the boat—would've tackled the storm differently too, but that's another story—anyway, it all got violent, and people started shooting—"

"In the middle of a storm? While you're taking on water?" Annalie asked incredulously.

"Yep. I think if they abandoned the ship they wouldn't get another one, so they had powerful reasons to stay, but some of them were convinced they were going to go under. Anyway, some of them decided to stay and shoot it out, but the captain gave the order to abandon ship, and they took me with them. So there we were, in a horrendous storm, ten people jammed into one lifeboat, and the lifeboat was being smashed by waves, and things kept getting washed overboard. We had no water, we had no food, the emergency beacon was gone. It's the Moon Islands, and we're in the middle of nowhere. Some of the guys were hoping our boat would come back and pick us up, but the others said there was no chance: if they'd managed to survive the storm without sinking the boat or shooting each other dead, they'd be heading for the nearest safe port and claiming the boat as booty. Apparently that's how they do things in the Kang Brotherhood: once you get a boat, you fight to the death to hang onto it, and let your shipmates look out for themselves.

"Anyway, no one came for us, and we didn't see anybody. We drifted for days. Then one of the crew said, 'Why are we keeping this guy around? He's not one of us and he's just one more mouth to feed.' The captain said, 'When we get him to land he's worth money, and we're going to need it.' They all started arguing about whether they should keep me alive or not. I tried to convince them to keep me: 'I can help you, I'll catch fish, I know how to make fresh water.' So I built a solar still, but they were too impatient to let it work properly, then someone knocked it over and the fresh water got mixed back in with the salt water, so the captain said, 'I've had enough of this. Let's throw him overboard.' Well, that was bad enough, but then someone else said, 'Now let's not be too hasty. He's an old bloke, but he's still got a bit of meat on him.'"

Annalie squeaked. "They were going to eat you?"

"Raw?" Will added.

"Spinner sashimi," Spinner said. "Some of them didn't like the idea at first, but then they started to come round to it, so I decided it was time to go."

"What did you do?" asked Annalie.

"When it was dark, I stole a life jacket and went overboard. I floated in the dark all night, and I was afraid the whole time that something was going to come up from the deep and eat me. But nothing did. The next day I floated past a boat that picked me up. Fortunately they weren't pirates, and after they dropped me off I took a passage to Norlind to see

Sujana, then made my way south to see Vesh."

"Did you take the Trans-Northern Express?" asked Annalie.

"No," Spinner said, sounding puzzled. "It doesn't take you anywhere near Brundisi."

"I *knew* he was lying!" Annalie said. "Beckett told us he'd almost caught you on the Trans-Northern Express, but you fell off the train and got smashed to bits."

"He told you I was dead?" Spinner asked. "What a horrible thing to do."

"He was desperate," Will crowed. "He can't catch you and he can't catch us. But we knew he was faking."

"But you still haven't told us why you never answered our messages," Annalie said.

"The Kangs took my shell away on the first day and I never got it back," Spinner said. "They have a theory that the Admiralty secretly hijacked the technology so they can monitor every shell in the world. Sounds a bit unlikely to me—do they really have the resources to do that?— but you never know, they could be right. Anyway, I've never really used the thing that much, so I didn't really think about it until Vesh showed me that story about my children the kidnappers. Anyway, I'm sorry. I had no idea you'd been trying to reach me. From now on, I'll try to be more contactable."

"Contactable is good," Will said. "But findable is even better. Don't go *anywhere* until we get there, okay? We're on our way to see you!"

The Sea of Brundisi

Before the Flood, Brundisi was a big country with dramatic geography—huge mountains, a vast river, fertile countryside—and an enormous population who spoke many different languages. Once, Brundisi had been a patchwork of kingdoms and clans, republics and fiefdoms, but gradually it had coalesced into a more or less coherent nation; it had grown rich on its goldfields, its abundant agricultural output, and later, on its factories, which churned out every item imaginable.

The Brundisi that arrived on the world scene in the hundred years or so before the Flood was energetic, abundant, and ever-growing as it tried to drag its enormous population out of rural poverty and into the kind of wealth and comfort that countries like Dux and the nations of the north enjoyed. But Brundisi was unlucky. The geography that had made it rich—the great river, fed by snowmelt in the high mountains, and its fertile floodplain, where all the crops were grown—also made it vulnerable. As the world grew warmer, the snow stopped falling in the high mountains; the snowmelt stopped feeding the river; the river began to dry out. The rains stopped too, and soon there was not enough water to drink or grow food. Hundreds of millions of people lived in Brundisi. As the price of food and water skyrocketed, riots broke out.

The Brundisan government held talks with other governments about what could be done, but the other governments had their own problems with food and water and riots; they didn't offer much help.

Extraordinary measures began to seem reasonable. Water was the problem. They had once had water, and now it was gone. Was there anything they could do to get it back?

Then a small team of scientists announced that they had discovered a way to release some of the water back into the system. They called it the Collodius Process.

No one really took the scientists very seriously. They were a small team, from a small country, at a not-very-prestigious university. There wasn't an outcry when they published details of their process in a scientific journal. The few people who took any notice of it—a few scientists, a few politicians—thought it was nonsense. One or two of these scientists said that if you ever attempted such a thing the results could be catastrophic, but most of them didn't. They simply thought it wouldn't work.

But someone in the Brundisi government had noticed. They were willing to give it a try. They summoned the scientists to Brundisi and gave them a lab to work in. The team built a prototype of the device. They tested it in secret; it worked. The Brundisi government decided to take it to the next level. They let the scientists announce their success as a prelude to the next round: a live test, in real conditions.

More people paid attention this time; a few leading scientists warned them not to do anything stupid. A few ambassadors were asked to tell the Brundisi government to back off. But even now, the level of urgency was not that high. With all the other things that were going on in the world—famines and water wars—a live test of a dubious new scientific process seemed like the least of anyone's worries.

The Flood was the result. Brundisi itself suffered torrential rain for weeks. The country was devastated by flooding. The loss of life was staggering. The problem spread wider, became a global event, became the Flood. And at the end of it, the original problem had not been solved. The snow didn't return; the river wasn't saved. Brundisi was wrecked, and the rest of the world, furious about what they had done, turned their backs on them.

The country the *Sunfish* was sailing toward was truly a disaster area. The Sea of Brundisi had risen particularly high in the Flood, swamping great tracts of coastal land. The wreckage of the old Brundisi extended several miles out to sea, the factories, the apartment blocks, the railroads and bridges and flyovers turning to decaying hulks of corroded concrete and rusting steel, a vast barrier to shipping of all kinds. Brundisi was now one of the poorest nations on earth, so they had never attempted to clear away the wreckage, as other, richer countries had.

Vesh—Ganaman Kiveshalan—lived somewhere near the coast in the city of Dio. The address they had for him was not really an address at all; rather like Sujana's, it was a set of directions for how to get somewhere, rather than a place you could simply look up on the links. Annalie had discussed how to get there with Spinner as they planned their final approach, and he had given them some useful tips about how to find their way.

"You do know about the Sea of Brundisi, don't you?" Spinner asked as Annalie finished making notes about the route. The four friends were sitting round the table in the saloon, Annalie's shell on speaker.

"What about it?" she asked.

"There are a lot of pirates here."

"Oh," Annalie said. "Yes."

"We've run into pirates before," said Will. "The proper ones down in the Moon Islands with the massive gunships. Aren't these just guys in dinghies with a bad attitude?"

"And automatic weapons," Spinner said. "Don't underestimate them. If you see anyone like that coming toward you, get out of there. Okay?"

"We can handle it," Will said. "In fact, I've been doing a bit of work on the motor. I think you'll be pretty impressed when you see what it can do."

Spinner chuckled. "Just make sure you get here in one piece."

Despite Spinner's warning, their journey along the coast of Brundisi was uneventful, and they soon reached the place where the *Sunfish* would wait while Will and Annalie went ashore. To a casual observer, the debris field seemed to extend unbroken in both directions up and down the coast, but Spinner had explained that there was, in fact, a channel running through it which was big enough to allow decent-sized boats to come in to shore, and once they were upon it they could see that the way was actually quite clear. The *Sunfish* could probably have sailed up it without any difficulty and found a mooring somewhere much closer to shore, but Spinner had advised against it. "I'd rather not leave the boat lying around where people can look at it and get ideas," he'd said. So they'd agreed to drop anchor at the opening of the channel where they could easily escape to open sea if they needed to.

Annalie called Spinner as they were preparing to step aboard the dinghy. He didn't answer, so she left him a message: "Hey, Spinner, we're here. We're coming ashore, okay? Can't wait to see you!"

She stashed her shell, wrapped in plastic, into an inside pocket and turned to look at Pod and Essie. "Well," she said, "this is it."

"Good luck," Essie said.

"We won't need luck," Will said. "He'll probably be there on the shore waiting for us."

"This is so exciting!" Essie said. "I can't wait to meet him."

"Be careful over there," Pod said. "This place sounds bad."

"You think every place sounds bad," Will said.

"I'm usually right," Pod said.

There were hugs all round, and then Will and Annalie climbed down the ladder and into the dinghy.

Will looked at Annalie. "This could be the end of the journey," he said.

"We've thought that before," Annalie said.

"I know," Will said. "But this time, if he's not there, I'm seriously going to kill him." He grinned as he gunned the engine, and together they headed for the darkening shore.

They followed the deep water channel, moving through outlying debris toward the half-sunken townscape.

"Remind you of anywhere?" Will asked.

"Sure does," Annalie said.

At the town's outer edges, the houses were little more than stubs, broken down and washed away by forty years of ocean storms. It looked a lot like Saltytown, the outer edge of the sprawling slum where Will and Annalie had grown up. As they wound their way up the channel and the water grew shallower, there were more and more intact houses where the signs of daily life flourished: smoke rose from chimneys, washing hung from lines, solar panels and turbines jutted from rooftops. The people here—and there were clearly a *lot* of people here—had stayed and made the best of things, just as they had in Will and Annalie's home in Lowtown (the more habitable part of the slum). Here, as there, most of them probably had little choice.

The channel was busy: dinghies prowled up and down, motors roaring; little skiffs were poled about; and there were larger boats drifting along under a single sail. A large-ish merchant boat churned past them, heading out to sea, proving that the channel was deep enough to admit quite large vessels. Will kept an eye out as they passed through, remembering Spinner's warnings about pirates, and he saw a few people stop and watch them as they passed. But he couldn't tell whether there was hostility in it or just ordinary curiosity.

The channel curved, following an organic sort of path that made it seem that it had once been a river. It was not really possible to see far ahead, and so they had very little warning as they came round a bend into an open harbor and saw a boat that was quite unlike all the other vessels sitting at anchor. It was sleek and new and powerful, crowned with an expensive array of high-tech equipment, and it was sitting at anchor directly in their path.

It was an Admiralty pursuit ship.

Will instantly turned the dinghy around and went motoring back the way they'd come.

"What are they doing here?" Annalie said, her heart pounding.

"I don't want to find out," Will said grimly. "We're going to have to find another way in to shore. If this place is anything like home, there'll be other ways."

Back home he'd been taught the secret back ways through the Eddy. Here, he'd just be making it up as he went along. But there was no way he was crossing that water in full view of an Admiralty pursuit ship.

"Do you think they've been tracking us?" Annalie asked, worried. "Or Spinner?"

"What difference does it make?" Will said. "We just need to find him before they do." He paused, watching where the local boat traffic was going, hoping to pick up some ideas about which way to go. "When we get to shore, do you know where we need to go?" he asked.

Annalie checked her directions and her map, then looked up at the townscape. "That way," she said, pointing.

"Then we'll go that way," Will said.

He dropped the engine to a crawl and took them down a flooded side street. The streets did not follow an orderly plan; they turned and twisted and wandered into dead ends. It would be very easy to get lost or disoriented here. Will puttered on, doing his best to stay on course; Annalie was keeping an eye on her compass to make sure they were going in more or less the right direction. One street they went down was blocked by a house that had collapsed into the middle of it; they had to turn and go back. On another street, a dinghy fell in behind them and followed them up the street, matching their pace. Just as Annalie was starting to get worried, they reached the end of the street and turned into the next one. The other dinghy broke off, apparently satisfied that it had seen them off, and turned back.

At last they reached a place where the streets sloped upward and the sea ended. Many little boats of all kinds were pulled up here; Will and Annalie tied the dinghy up, Will disabled the engine so no one could steal it, and they stepped onto dry land.

"Let's find Spinner," Will said.

Spinner had given them a series of landmarks to navigate by: "Walk toward the white tower; find the canal and follow it until you reach the third bridge; cross over. On the other side of the canal there's some open ground. Cross that; on the other side of it there are some factories and warehouses. Look for the old sports shoe factory—you can't miss it, there's a huge sports shoe on a pole above the gate."

They walked. It was already late in the afternoon, but they were unwilling to put off this last part of the journey until tomorrow. Why would they wait, when they were so close? Around them the busy day was in full swing and the streets were teeming with people. They found the white tower without too much trouble; it was tall enough to catch the late afternoon sun glowing across the city. A large market spread out from the foot of the tower, selling everything from fresh produce to shoes and old bits of tech, and everywhere there were stalls selling delicious-smelling food that made Will's mouth water.

"Do you suppose we've got time to get a quick bite?" he suggested, looking longingly at a dumpling stall.

"I'd be surprised if they take Duxish money," Annalie said, although she wouldn't have minded a little something.

"Maybe Spinner can get us something later," Will sighed.

They kept walking reluctantly past the food stalls and continued on through the market, which was very large and confusingly laid out.

"What are we looking for next? The canal?" Will asked.

"Yes," Annalie said. She stopped and was reaching into her pocket for her shell when Will put a hand on her arm.

"Look," he said. "Marines."

Still some distance away from them, they saw a pair of Admiralty marines. They had stopped a man and were questioning him—it looked like they were asking him for his papers. The man was not wearing Brundisan clothes and had a vaguely northern look.

"Reckon they're stopping and searching anyone who doesn't look local?" Annalie said.

"Uh-huh," Will said.

They backed away from the two marines, hoping to be inconspicuous, but then a strong Duxish voice rang out behind them—"Hey!"—and they knew they'd been seen.

Will grabbed Annalie and dragged her between two stalls, and the two of them began ducking and weaving through the market, running on instinct. No one seemed very inclined to point them out to the pursuing marines, and after only a few minutes the shouts had faded and the marines were nowhere to be seen. They hid behind a stall that sold bedspreads to catch their breath.

"Do you think they were looking for us?" Annalie said. "Or Spinner?"

"I don't know," Will said, "but we'd better warn him. And the others."

Annalie tried to call Spinner; he didn't answer. She left him a message, then sent another to Essie and

Pod: *The Admiralty are here and they're looking for someone. BE CAREFUL.*

"What do we do now?" Annalie asked.

"Try and find that canal," Will said.

"Are they coming back?" Pod asked when Essie had read out their message.

"I don't think so," Essie said. "I guess they haven't found Spinner yet."

Pod looked gloomily out to sea. "Everywhere we go, the Admiralty follows us. How do they keep doing that?"

"Well, they do have a huge fleet, political power, tons of money, and the very best technology in the world on their side," Essie said. "But they haven't got what we've got."

"What's that?"

"Agility, determination, and a talking parrot." Essie grinned.

The talking parrot spoke up. "Engine!" he rasped.

It took a moment for either of them to realize what Graham had said. "Did you say 'engine'?" Pod asked.

"Stupid Pod. Listen!" Graham said.

They listened, and as usual, Graham was right. The distant whine of an outboard motor was carrying in bursts across the water toward them.

Pod grabbed the binoculars. He scanned the horizon, failing to see anything at first. The sound grew louder.

"There!" shouted Essie.

A small boat was moving toward them. Pod looked at it through the binoculars.

"What is it?" Essie asked.

"Guys in a dinghy," Pod said. "With automatic weapons."

Guys in a dinghy

There were two men in the dinghy, weaving through the water toward them. It took a moment for Pod to realize that this must be because there were obstacles in the water.

"We'd better get out of here," Essie said.

"I'll try," Pod said. "But this is their home turf. They know what's down there. We don't."

Pod told Essie to bring up the anchor while he hurried to get the sails down and take the wheel. They had no chance of escaping under sail; they had to hope their motor was equal to the outboard on the zippy little dinghy.

They drove out toward the open sea, and for a few moments it seemed like they might simply be able to pull away from their pursuers. But the dinghy was faster. It came flashing across their bows, forcing Pod to spin the wheel.

"What are they doing?" cried Essie.

"Trying to drive us in toward shore," Pod said. There was nothing he could do; he steered away from the surging dinghy and the two men on board, armed with automatic weapons, and into the debris field.

Pod knew how to steer the boat, and had done so on many occasions, but never like this. Until now the really scary sailing had fallen to Will, and Pod was terrified that he was going to mess it up and sink them. "Keep a lookout!" he yelled.

Essie rushed to the bow to look out for underwater hazards. "I can see a lot of stuff up ahead," she warned.

"Just tell me when to turn!"

The dinghy was driving them ever deeper into the debris field. Pod twisted and turned, with Essie shouting directions from the bow, but the dinghy was faster and more maneuverable and kept sweeping in and cutting them off. The water was full of menace: dark shapes lurked beneath the water, and spars and spikes and lumps and projections stuck out all over the place. Pod realized the dinghy, with its much shallower draft, could easily ride over obstacles that would snag the *Sunfish*.

"There's something on the right!" Essie called.

Pod adjusted slightly.

"And on the left!" Essie called. "I'm going to need a pole!"

The *Sunfish* was sliding between two dark shapes below the surface. Pod did his best to steer a straight course as the boat skimmed between the two. Essie grabbed a pole, ready to fend off.

"We're getting awfully close on this side!" Essie called, straining with the effort as she shoved in her pole and tried to push the boat away from the underwater shape.

"Are we through?" Pod called.

"Yes, but there's more up ahead!" Essie said. "This is a maze!"

"I'm going to make a break for it," Pod said. He steered toward open sea again and pushed the engine harder.

At once the dinghy came zooming after them, cutting them off once again. Both guys were shouting at them furiously, and the one who wasn't driving threatened them with his weapon. They couldn't understand what he was saying, but the meaning was fairly clear: *Surrender, or I'll shoot.*

"Maybe we should try and talk to them," Essie called, frightened, as the barrel of the gun waved in her direction.

"You speak Brundisi?" Pod asked.

"No."

"How's that going to work, then?" Pod said. He aimed the *Sunfish* directly at the little dinghy and drove at it, full speed. The dinghy whipped out of the way, easily avoiding getting rammed, but the two men were really annoyed now. A quick burst of gunfire split the air, shockingly loud.

"They're shooting at us!" Essie squeaked.

"Did they hit us?" Pod yelled.

"Don't think so," Essie said. "Shots went wide."

"Let's get out of here," Pod said.

He kept going on the line that he'd chosen, the engine working at top speed. Essie turned back to watch the men in the dinghy who kept whizzing around them, changing position, shouting and threatening.

Pod noticed what she was doing and shouted, "Don't watch them! Look ahead!"

Essie turned again, and saw to her horror another looming shape in the water. "There's something dead ahead!"

Pod adjusted his heading, but they were too close, and going too fast. They stuck on something, hard. The boat shuddered and they heard a horrible crunch. The engine roared harder, but the boat was going nowhere.

"What's happened? Go see!" Pod yelled, and Essie went scampering down below to see if they were holed.

Pod revved the engine, hoping they might motor off, but it had no effect. The ocean swell started to slap against them.

Pod left the wheel and went to grab Essie's pole, hoping he might be able to push them off, but he ran right around the boat and could see nothing to push against. Whatever they'd hit, it was underneath.

Essie came hurrying back up. "There's no water coming in," she said. "I can't see a hole."

"We must have snagged the keel or the steering," Pod said.

The engine was still roaring, fruitlessly. He powered it down.

The dinghy guys were grinning now, circling in toward them.

"What are we going to do?" Essie asked.

"Maybe I can take them out with the speargun again," Pod said.

"Wait," Essie said. "I've got another idea." She slipped below.

The dinghy was alongside them now. The guy in the bow, who was wearing huge mirrored sunglasses, shouted at Pod and indicated he should put his hands up. His friend had his gun trained on him and he didn't look afraid to use it. Pod put his hands up.

Mr. Sunglasses shouted at Pod a bit more, waving at him to take a step back. Then he went to the ladder at the back of the *Sunfish* and began to climb up, the driver still covering him with the gun. Pod waited for Mr. Sunglasses to appear, his heart thumping. He'd already let the *Sunfish* be captured once. He couldn't let the same thing happen again. He scanned the deck for possible weapons, his brain moving at a million miles an hour, trying to calculate his chances of success if he simply rushed the guy as he came over the side. He might be able to take out one guy, but the other one had the gun. What could he do about him? And Essie was nowhere to be seen. Whatever her idea was, he hoped it was a good one.

Mr. Sunglasses appeared at the top of the ladder, his mirrored lenses flashing in the sunlight. He grinned as he looked around the deck, savoring his prize. And then, just as suddenly, Pod heard a cry and then a splash. Mr. Sunglasses had vanished.

He whipped round and saw Essie standing there, the slingshot in her hand. She grinned at him, and for a moment Pod stared at her incredulously. But there was no time for explanations. The driver shouted in rage and fear and aimed a spray of bullets at them. Pod and Essie hit the deck as the driver went to retrieve his friend from the water. Mr. Sunglasses was unconscious, and already starting to sink. The driver blasted another spray at them, then dragged his friend into the dinghy as quickly as possible. He was just turning to give them a third spray when Essie popped up again, slingshot at the ready, and let loose another stone. It hit the driver squarely on the forehead with a loud, horrible *donk*, and he toppled over sideways onto his friend.

"Woah," Pod said, impressed. "When did you learn to do that?"

"On the island," Essie said.

Pod laughed and shook his head. "Man, you've changed," he said.

Essie took this as praise.

"So, what are we going to do about those guys?" she asked.

"We should tip them both into the water," Pod said.

"We can't do that!" Essie said, horrified.

"They were trying to kill us," Pod said.

"They were trying to capture us and steal our boat," Essie said. "It's different. We can't kill them."

"What do you think they're going to do to us when they wake up?" Pod said.

"We just need to make sure we're far, far away from them," Essie said.

"Okay, fine," Pod said. "But we're definitely taking those guns."

"One thing I learned from vids," Essie said, "is that if you have a gun and you don't know how to use it, the bad guys are just going to take it off you and use it against you."

"Who says I don't know how to use a gun?" Pod said stubbornly.

"I bet Annalie wouldn't want guns on the boat," Essie said.

"I bet Will would," Pod said.

"Okay, we'll find somewhere to hide the guns until they get back," Essie said, "and then we can decide what to do with them. But going back to the first question: what are we going to do with those guys?"

The two men were still lying on the bottom of the dinghy, unmoving.

"You don't think you killed them already, do you?" Pod asked.

"I couldn't have," Essie said, appalled.

"I'd better go and see," Pod said.

He clambered down the ladder and stepped into the dinghy ever so cautiously. It rocked under his weight, but the men didn't move. Pod reached for the nearest gun and eased it out of the pirate's inert hand, then passed it up to Essie. She took it unwillingly. The second rifle was buried somewhere underneath the two prone bodies. He felt around under them, afraid that at any moment one of them might wake up and grab him. He winkled out the second gun, and it followed the first one up onto the deck of the *Sunfish*.

"Better check that they're okay," Essie said.

Pod made a face at her, but he gingerly put a hand on first one neck, then the other, looking for a pulse. "They're still breathing," he said.

"So now what do we do with them?" Essie asked.

Pod looked around him at the empty ocean, looking for inspiration. There was no one else in sight, and the distant shore seemed deserted.

"I reckon we just point them toward land," he said. He started the dinghy's engine again, leaving it on its lowest purr, pointed the prow toward the shore, and let it go, jumping back aboard the *Sunfish* as the dinghy puttered away.

"I hope they don't have too many friends," Essie said.

"Let's get out of here before we have to find out," Pod said.

"We have to get the boat unstuck first," Essie said. "Let's go and see what's happened."

Breathe

A second internal inspection did not reveal any signs of water coming in, so Pod and Essie felt reasonably confident the hull was intact. That meant something underneath the boat must have been snagged. And someone would have to go down there and have a look.

Normally this would have been a job for Will. He loved to dive, using just a mask and flippers. He never used a snorkel—he didn't even own one.

"I wish Will was here," Essie said.

"But he's not," Pod said.

"It can't wait until he gets back."

"No."

Essie looked at Pod, knowing full well he couldn't swim. She could, although she didn't really fancy diving down into underwater wreckage. The thought of getting tangled down there gave her the horrors. But she couldn't see any alternative.

"I'll go," she said.

They were lucky that they were in the Sea of Brundisi, which was much farther south than Norlind. An underwater inspection off the coast of Norlind would have been impossible. Here, it would be cold, but it wouldn't actually kill you in minutes.

Essie strapped on the flippers and mask, then it was a bracing drop into the cold water, and her whole skin seemed to contract in shock. She hung there on the surface, not at all sure that she could do this, but then she reminded herself that everyone was counting on her. She took a couple of deep breaths, filled her lungs, and plunged.

Down she went, down under the boat. It didn't take long to see what had happened. Below them was a hunk of slanting, twisted concrete and metal, warped beyond recognition. Large spars stuck up here and there out of the concrete, and one of these had become entangled with their steering. The good news was they were not badly stuck on the spar, and the metal was old and rusty. A more serious problem was the steering itself. It looked to Essie—although she could not spend long examining it, as she felt like her lungs were already about to burst—as if the steering had been buckled and damaged. She suspected they would not be going anywhere until one of them could do something to repair it.

She swam for the surface, stars popping in front of her eyes. It took her a few moments to get enough breath back before she could speak.

"What did you see?" asked Pod.

"I think it's the steering that's caught," she said. "It should be pretty easy to get us free, but the bigger problem is going to be fixing it."

"There's no easy way to get the steering out of

the assembly and fix it while we're out at sea," Pod said. "We'd need to get the boat into dry dock. But I don't know where we can do that round here. Can we get by without repairs?"

"I'm no expert," Essie said, "but it doesn't look good."

They both sat for a moment, wondering what to do next.

"You say it shouldn't be too hard to get us free," Pod said. "Let's do that first and then worry about the steering. Maybe it's not as bad as you think."

"Maybe," Essie said, although she didn't feel hopeful.

Pod turned to Graham, who had been watching all this with polite interest. "Graham, you're our lookout," he said. "If you see any signs of more guys in dinghies coming from the shore, you let me know, okay?"

Graham *skrarked* affirmatively and flew off to the top of the mast to keep watch.

"Do you think you can do this?" Pod asked.

"I don't know," Essie said. "I'll try." She looked down into the water, anxiety tugging at her. "Only thing is, I don't know how long I can hold my breath for. It might take me a few goes before I can actually get us free."

Pod looked down at the water too, considering the problem.

"My first job," he said, "they sent us down into flooded places to find stuff. We took a hose down, breathed through that."

"Do we have a hose?" Essie asked.

"There's the one we use for filling the water tanks," Pod said. "And I can rig up the bilge pump to pump air instead."

"Okay," Essie said. "Let's do it."

Aware that at any moment more pirates could come after them from the shore of Brundisi, which now seemed painfully close by, the two of them set to work. While Pod attached the hose to the pump, Essie put together a toolkit of everything she might need and put it into a plastic bag rigged with a flotation device so it wouldn't sink under its own weight.

"Okay," Pod said. "Are you sure you can do this?"

"Do I have a choice?" Essie said.

"Of course," Pod said, frowning. "If you don't want to go down there—"

"It's okay. I'll be fine," Essie said.

And she went back into the water before she could change her mind.

She paused on the surface, practicing breathing through the hose. They'd added a strap to it so she could keep it near her face and breathe through it hands-free. Air bubbled through it continuously; the stream of bubbles was quite distracting, so she decided to push it to one side of her face and just grab it for a breath whenever she needed it.

"Okay," she shouted, "I'm going down!"

She descended. The underwater landscape was more than a little creepy, with dark shapes and hollows everywhere filled with algae and weeds. There could be anything lurking down there in those vast, post-industrial hidey-holes. She tried not to think about sharks.

The first thing to do was disentangle the steering from the spar. Essie had already decided to do this the low-tech way: she grabbed a hammer from the bag of tools and began to smash it. The spar had been in the water for forty years; it could not survive that kind of punishment for long. After no more than a minute or two of smashing (and several bubbly breaths grabbed from the hose), the top of the spar broke off and the *Sunfish* floated free.

Essie swam for the surface, pleased with herself. "We're off!" she shouted.

"Great!" Pod said, helping her back on board. "Let's see if we can steer."

He started the engine and tried to turn the boat out toward open water once again. But the steering was clearly jammed; the boat wouldn't steer to the left or right.

"It's no good," Pod said. "If we can't turn, we can't get out of the debris field."

"I'm going to have to try and unjam it, aren't I?" Essie said.

Pod gave her an uncomfortable look. She knew the situation; Pod couldn't swim, but more than that, he was afraid of the water. She couldn't possibly expect him to go down there. "It's okay," she said. "Hopefully it won't be too tricky."

Essie prepared herself again and went down for a second time. The underwater landscape had changed, and she realized belatedly that they were drifting.

Probably, she thought, they should have anchored while she made repairs. She thought about going back up and telling Pod, but decided not to bother. It would only be wasting time, and if the pirates came back unexpectedly it would be better if they could get away quickly.

She took a breath from the bubbling hose and studied the rudder. The light under the boat was green and dim and she wished she had a flashlight, but as she peered at it she thought she could see what the problem was. Essie had never looked at a rudder up close and had no idea what it was supposed to look like, but she could see two things: a chunk of the metal spar remained wedged between the rudder and the assembly; and the rudder itself had twisted a little on its axis. If she could get the piece of metal out, that might fix the problem, although the twist might present further problems. But first things first. She would try and get the metal out.

She whanged it with her trusty hammer, and managed to break some of the projecting piece off, but a chunk of it was left behind, and she quickly realized she couldn't do any more whacking without risking damaging the rudder. She opened the bag and tried to slide the hammer back inside, but somehow missed the opening. The hammer dropped straight down into the murky green depths. Essie, panicked, dived down after it, forgetting about the hose that was attached to her mask strap. She knew how precious tools were—she couldn't lose the hammer! She kicked down, reaching for it. Her hand closed around it—and the stream of bubbles at her ear ceased.

Up on deck, Pod heard the pop as the hose came free from the pump. His heart pounding, he tried to grab for it, but the hose had already whisked over the side and down into the sea. He leaned over the water as far as he dared, but of course he could see nothing in the dark water below.

"Essie!" he shouted, although he knew it was pointless.

Bubbles were rolling up from the deep. He watched them in horror, not knowing what to do. Should he dive in after her? What was going on down there? He remembered the day his best friend had been sent down searching for salvage in an old factory; he'd had a better breathing tube than this one, but the pump had malfunctioned and his friend had drowned down there, lost in the dark. They'd brought the body up so it wouldn't attract predators. He still dreamed of being caught in dark places underwater, unable to breathe. Had he sent Essie down to meet the same fate?

Just as he thought this, Essie burst suddenly onto the surface, gasping, a hammer clutched in her hand, the hose dangling.

"What happened?" he called, his relief immense.

"Dropped the hammer," Essie said. "I forgot about the hose."

She clambered up on deck and shivered, trying to warm up, while Pod worked to reattach the hose. Graham flew down beside them.

"Engine broken?" he asked.

"The engine's fine, but we need to fix the steering."

"Why send her?" Graham asked. "Pod good fixer."

"Thanks," Essie said.

"I can't go down there," Pod said. "I can't swim."

"Don't swim. Just fix."

Pod looked at Graham angrily. "If it's so easy, maybe you should do it."

"We've all got jobs to do," Essie said. "Wasn't yours looking out for pirates?"

Graham nipped her toe and flew off to the top of the mast again.

"I've got this," Essie said. "Are we ready?"

"We're ready," Pod said.

Back in the water she went, down and down into the murky green depths. The boat floated above her, and a gentle swell kept things rolling and moving. Luckily they were in a relatively clear patch now, but she realized that yet again she had come down without remembering to tell Pod to anchor them in one place. She returned to the rudder and pulled some pliers out of the bag with exaggerated care (she did not want to risk dropping anything else). With one hand she braced herself against the *Sunfish*'s hull, and with the other she tried to get a good grip on the metal with the pliers and winkle the metal free. She tugged and teased, treading water with her legs to try and stay in one spot while the bubbles streamed about her, occasionally getting in her face as she worked. She felt the metal give, and she was ready to rejoice, but then she realized that the metal had separated, and some of it was still in there. She tried to get a grip on the remaining piece with the pliers.

A big wave rolled through. The boat moved, Essie

moved, the debris stayed where it was, and suddenly Essie felt an agonizing pain. She had washed into more debris, and a projecting metal spike had stabbed right into her thigh. For a moment she thought she was actually impaled, but then she skidded free with a painful scrape. In her panic she swallowed water and raced for the surface, coughing and spluttering, afraid for her life.

Pod was there at once, looking down at her. "What's wrong?"

"There was a wave," she sputtered. "I crashed into something—"

"Are you hurt?"

Essie filled her lungs with soothing air, trying to still her racing heart. "My leg," she said. "Something stabbed me."

"How bad is it?"

She put her mask under the water to look at the wound. Blood was blooming around her. "Oh dear," she said.

Pod put out a hand and quickly hauled her back up.

"I don't think it's that bad," she gabbled, her heart still racing. "I should go back down. I've almost fixed it, at least I think I have. One more try ought to do it—ow!"

Pod was wiping the blood away, trying to see the extent of the injury. Her thigh had been scraped raw, and although the graze was quite large, it was not particularly bad. But there was one long, deep wound that looked nasty, and it was bleeding profusely.

"You can't go back down there," Pod said. "Not with that."

"It's not that bad—" Essie began.

"Blood in the water brings sharks," Pod said. "Don't you know anything?"

He was scowling. Essie thought he was angry at her, but then he started working at the knots that held the rope around her waist.

"What are you doing?" Essie asked.

"I have to go down there and finish the job."

"Pod—no—"

"I have to."

"I can go—"

"No, you can't. Give me the mask."

Essie could see there was no point arguing with him. She took off the mask. "There's just a little bit of metal stuck between the rudder and the assembly. You might need the pliers to get it out or you might be able to just force it out with something narrow like a screwdriver."

Pod nodded, although she wasn't sure he was really listening.

"If you can't handle it down there, just come up, come straight back up, and we'll work out another plan. Will and Annalie will probably be back soon and they can help us. It's all going to be okay."

"We can't wait," Pod said. "I have to do this."

He sat on the metal step that projected from the stern for a moment or two, steeling himself, and then he went over the side.

Pod underwater

Pod could count on one hand the number of times he'd been in the water since he was sold on from that first terrible job. There was the time he and Essie had jumped off the *Blue Water Princess*, and the time he and Will escaped from angry islanders back in the Moon Islands. Before that, there was the time his pirate captain had thrown him off the ship to drown. All of them had been terrifying experiences. But none of them felt quite the same as this one.

He floated on the surface, up to his neck in seawater, the horrible depths below him, the air hose hissing at his ear.

"Just put your head under and practice breathing first," Essie said. "It takes a bit of getting used to, but you can do it."

But Pod knew exactly how to do it. He'd done it before, as a child. He'd had no choice. The memories came back now—all of them. Not just how to breathe through a bubbling hose. But how it felt to have that water pressing down upon you. How it felt to be creeping through the drowned ruins of someone else's world. The fear and the anger he sometimes felt at how badly the people before them had messed things up, so that people had to live like this.

But none of this was helping him. He tried to ram it all down into a place where he didn't have to feel it or think about it, and reminded himself that he just had to do the next thing. Put one foot in front of the other. Take this step, then the next step. That's how you go on.

He went down under, really under. The water bubbled at his ear and he gulped a breath. Down the sloping hull, down to the rudder, a rope paying out behind him, tethering him to the surface. He peered at the rudder and saw at once what needed to be done. He took the pliers out, positioned himself carefully, then worked the last piece of metal gently back and forth, back and forth, until at last it slipped free, as easy as anything. He ran his hands over the rudder and its axis, wondering how bad the damage was. Essie was right, the rudder was twisted. But would it prevent them from steering? He couldn't tell. He fished out the hammer from the bag and gave the rudder a knock to see if he could straighten it out. It didn't seem to make a lot of difference, but as soon as he'd done it, he thought better of it. The metal had already been twisted and strained. He didn't want to risk weakening it even further and having it snap right off under pressure.

He put the hammer back in its bag. He had done as much as he could do. The job was done. He could return to the surface.

He grabbed the rope and hauled himself up, hand

over hand, back up the curve of the boat and into the sunlight.

Essie stuck her head over anxiously. "Are you okay?"

"It's done. I fixed it."

"Already?"

"Didn't take much."

She put out a hand to him and helped him out of the water. Pod sat on the metal shelf, his feet still dangling. "I'm dizzy," he said.

"It's the hose, it's hard to breathe, isn't it?"

"No—it's not that." He ripped off the mask and hose and threw them away from him. "I didn't think I could do that."

"Well, you did," Essie said.

For a moment longer he didn't move, still staring into the water. Graham flew down beside him and rubbed his wet leg with his beak. "Silly Pod. No more water now."

Pod smiled at him and stroked his blue head. "Dead right. No more water."

The old sports shoe factory

"I think we're lost," Annalie said.

They were still trying to find the canal. It had taken them quite some time to get out of the market: the passages between the stalls were narrow and crooked, so they kept on walking in circles, and they'd had to keep hiding from Admiralty marines. When they did finally manage to get out, they'd found themselves lost in a maze of streets that all seemed to look the same. Annalie's shell was less useful than it might have been elsewhere: the maps it contained had never been updated for these broken-down towns, so they showed streets and buildings that might have existed forty years ago but did not necessarily exist now—although some did, just to make it even more confusing.

"Treat it like an orienteering exercise," Will said, grumpy and frustrated. "Take a compass heading and we'll find it that way."

Although the shell's map was less than helpful about the streets or the route, it could show them where they were, and where the canal was. (They assumed that the canal, at least, had not moved.) If they worked out the right compass heading and just kept walking in that direction, they knew they'd eventually hit the canal. They began to walk.

"Spinner still hasn't called us back," Will said.

"I know," Annalie said. "Typical, huh?"

"What do you reckon his excuse'll be this time?"

Just as Annalie was about to say something on Spinner's behalf, her shell was snatched out of her hand. Annalie was so shocked that for a moment she couldn't even react, but Will's reflexes were quicker. He took off after the thief, roaring in fury, and Annalie hurried after him, her heart pounding. If they lost that shell, they lost their ability to contact Spinner and their friends back on the *Sunfish*. They had to get it back.

The thief was a boy, younger than themselves, quick and determined; but Will was quick and determined too, and extremely competitive. He shouldered and elbowed his way down the street, ignoring shouts and protests, bearing implacably down on the thief until at last he hurled himself onto the boy and knocked him flat. Annalie ran up to see her brother wrenching the shell from the boy's hand as he held him down.

"That's not yours," he said furiously. People were already turning to stare, questioning, looking hostile. Somebody shouted something at Will.

"This is ours!" he said. "We were just trying to get it back!"

More people were gathering around, accusing and gesticulating; to Will's fury, they seemed to think *he* was the villain. The boy, taking no chances, scampered away into the crowd.

282

Annalie grabbed Will and tugged him out of the knot of people, apologizing as she went. "We're sorry, we don't want any trouble, we're going now. Come on, Will!"

They pushed their way politely but firmly through the gathering crowd, knowing they couldn't afford to attract the attention of local law enforcement or those Admiralty marines. Angry people shouted and pointed fingers at them, but their interest in the situation seemed to be waning and they managed to escape without anyone placing them under a citizen's arrest.

"Didn't you bring a real compass?" Will asked.

Annalie had; she pulled it out of her pocket and showed it to him.

"Then what were you using your shell for?" he asked.

"I don't know. I didn't think," Annalie said. She was still rattled by how close she'd come to losing it.

Will shoved the shell back into her hand. "Keep it out of sight until we absolutely have to use it," he said.

They followed the compass's wavering needle through streets that were rapidly growing darker. The sun had almost set and this town, unlike the modern cities of Dux or the northlands, wasn't equipped with conveniences like streetlights. Individual shops and houses were strung with lights, but there were plenty of pools of darkness, and the streets were rough and uneven. They kept going, anxious and a little impatient at how long it was taking to find their way, but then a smell hit them: a noxious sewery smell of garbage, excrement, and rotten things.

"You reckon that's the canal?" Annalie said.

"Reckon it might be," Will said.

Gagging a little at the smell, they kept on, and soon they reached the canal. Houses backed onto it; some of it was fenced and some of it was not; garbage floated by. It was a truly revolting waterway.

"So we found it," Will said. "Now what?"

"We're supposed to cross the canal at the third bridge. Then there's some waste ground we have to cross to get to where Vesh lives."

They walked along the bank of the canal, which was littered with ankle-turning junk. A bridge loomed up out of the darkness.

"Shall we try this one?" Annalie asked.

Will was already halfway over it.

They found themselves in a vast, dark stretch of open ground. A few lights shone in the distance; they walked toward them, hoping this was the factory district where Vesh lived. The very last of the daylight was fading from the sky now, just a hint of an electric-blue glow, but at ground level no light remained. They walked over ground that gave slightly and sometimes squelched under their feet, acridly salty. The factory district, despite the lights that they could see here and there, was very dark. Clearly the factories no longer operated at night, if they operated at all. Their instructions hadn't mentioned whether these factories actually made anything, or whether they were ghost infrastructure left over from more prosperous times.

"How are we going to find a big shoe on a pole?" Will said as they got closer. "It's so dark."

"Maybe we should wait until the moon comes up," Annalie said.

"That's not for hours," Will said.

"Maybe when we get closer—"

Annalie didn't get to finish her sentence, for at that moment there was an almighty *boom*. The sky over the factory district lit up as the echo of the explosion rolled out across the fields and a huge fireball rolled up into the darkening sky, followed by a plume of smoke. Something began to glow, brighter and brighter. One of the factories was burning.

"Look!" Annalie said.

Silhouetted above the flames, she could see a pole thrusting up above the other buildings, and it had a shape on it that could well have been a giant sports shoe. As they watched, sparks landed on the shoe and blossomed suddenly into flame. The fire took hold of the shoe in an instant, burning fast and bright until it was consumed in a great rush. In moments there was nothing left but a tiny little stub at the top of the pole; then even that fell off and was gone.

"I have a bad feeling about this," Will said, and began to run toward the factories.

Annalie chased after him. "Will, wait! It's too dangerous!"

"Don't be stupid!" Will said furiously, and kept running.

Annalie knew, just as Will did, that the conjunction of Spinner and Vesh, the Admiralty pursuit ship, and the fire could not be an accident. They ran toward the flames, emerging from the salty field and into the streets again, and as they got closer they were caught up in a great press of humanity, some coming to help, others coming simply to gawk. The light from the fire burned brighter and brighter as they hurried through streets and alleyways, through the huge combustible old properties, until they reached the place they were looking for. The old sports shoe factory was alight. Huge sheets of flame rose from every window, generating a black pall of choking smoke.

Will and Annalie stopped and stared at the destruction in horror. Around them, people were trying to organize a bucket brigade to throw water on the flames, but it was pointless in the face of such a vast conflagration. The heat was so intense no one could get close enough to make a difference, and the smoke seemed to burn your eyes, your throat, even your skin, in a way that made you suspect this was not just ordinary smoke.

"What was Vesh's specialty?" Will asked.

"Chemistry," Annalie said.

Another fireball belched through the roof. Will grabbed Annalie and they ran back to what they hoped was a safer distance.

"What if they were inside?" Will asked.

Annalie couldn't answer. If they had been inside, there was no hope for them.

"Maybe the Admiralty arrested them," Annalie said, "and they're just burning the place down to teach them a lesson."

They stood in silence for a while longer, mesmerized and appalled by the flames. "Let's go round the perimeter," Will suggested finally. "Maybe they escaped. Maybe we'll see them. They can't be that hard to find, right?"

"Look," Annalie said.

Marines, spread out along the streets, watched the crowd intently. Were they looking for someone? Or were they simply trying to stop anyone from doing something to put out the fire?

"Let's just go," Annalie said, but Will could not be deterred.

"We can find them," he said. "We just have to try."

Will kept going, and Annalie followed, grief already starting to spill over inside her. They had asked Spinner to wait, and he had waited, and now...

She pulled her shell from her inside pocket, just in case. *No message. Nothing.*

Of course there wasn't.

Suddenly someone bumped into her. Shocked, she looked up to see a Brundisan woman staring at her intently. As Annalie opened her mouth to speak, the woman pressed something into her hand, closing Annalie's fingers tightly around it. Then she vanished into the crowd.

It was a piece of paper. Annalie looked at it, then chased after Will.

"Someone just gave me this! It could be a message!"

They stepped into the shadow of a doorway and Annalie unrolled the piece of paper. Her shell had a light in it; she shone it on the note.

"It's gibberish," Will said.

"It's code," Annalie said.

Quickly she snapped a picture of it and sent it to

Essie with a message: *Decipher this. Use the same key as the scientist list. Hurry.*

Essie's reply came straight back: *Will do.*

"Who gave you this?" Will asked.

"A local woman."

"Did she say anything?"

"Nope."

"Why didn't you stop her? She could have told us something!" Will snapped.

"It all happened so fast," Annalie protested. "She crashed into me, she gave me the message, then she was gone. I couldn't even tell you what she looked like."

"But if *he* gave her this message, she must know where he is."

"I know! I'm sorry, all right? Maybe the answers are in the message."

"They'd better be," Will said. He stepped out into the street again, staring at the crowd, still hoping a familiar face would come by. Annalie stood beside him, fear and anxiety twisting in her stomach.

Her shell rang and she snatched it up.

"It's me," Essie said. "I've decoded the message. It says: "The Admiralty are coming. Vesh and I are leaving. Do not come after me." That part's underlined. He says we need to go back to Dux and wait for him there and he'll be in touch."

"Go home? Like hell!" Will stormed.

"Wait, what is this message? What's going on?" Essie asked.

"I'll tell you later," Annalie said. "We're coming back." Ignoring Essie's protests, she hung up.

"So close!" Will groaned. "I can't believe it! How can we have missed him again?"

"I know," Annalie said, "but this is good news. They must have gotten advance warning somehow. He was able to send this note. Hopefully that means they got away."

"Yeah, you're right," Will said, his brow unknotting slightly.

"Let's get back to the *Sunfish*," Annalie said, "and work out what we're going to do next."

They were squelching their way back across the wasteland when the shell rang again. Annalie whipped it out; it was Spinner's number.

"Where are you?" she cried. "What happened?"

"You know my friend Beckett," Spinner said. His voice sounded tired. "He never gives up."

"We're here in Brundisi," Annalie said. "We saw the fire, we thought you were killed."

"I'm fine," Spinner said. "We got out before that happened. But listen, you two have got to stop this now. It's getting too dangerous. You have to go home, now, while you still can."

"But Spinner, we're right here!" Will jumped in. "You can't be that far away, not yet! We can come and meet you. We want to come with you!"

"You can't go where I'm going," Spinner said.

"Why not?" Annalie asked. "Where's that?"

"Sundia," Spinner said.

"But—haven't they closed their borders?" Will said. "I thought no one could go to Sundia."

"That's right," Spinner said.

"Then how're you getting there?"

"There are ways," Spinner said. "But it's not easy."

"Just let us come and meet you," Will said. "Just to see you. Please?"

"I can't let you," Spinner said. "I'm sorry."

"But we miss you," Annalie said, tears choking her. "We just want to see you."

"I want to see you too," Spinner said, his voice thick with emotion. "But it's impossible. Not right now, anyway. I promise, at the other end of this, we will be together. I'll find a way. But you've got to promise me you'll go home and stay safe. Promise me!"

Will and Annalie looked at each other.

"I promise we'll stay safe," Annalie said.

"Will?" Spinner prompted.

"Yeah. I promise," Will said grudgingly.

"I'm sorry about this. All of this," Spinner said. "I love you. I hope you know that."

"I love you too, Spinner," Annalie said, the tears spilling down her cheeks.

"Me too," Will said.

"I've got to go," Spinner said. "Keep your promise now, okay?"

"Okay," Annalie said.

And then he was gone.

Departures

"They're on their way back," Essie reported, as a message from Annalie flashed up on her shell.

Graham put his head up eagerly and crooned.

"Is everything okay? Have they got him?" Pod asked.

Essie looked at Graham and shook her head sorrowfully.

"No Spinner?" Graham said.

"I'm sorry," Essie said. "Annalie will explain."

Graham ruffled his feathers up miserably and turned his face to the wall.

Pod looked at Essie in a *what should I say?* sort of way. But Essie had nothing to offer. They could promise—again—that Spinner would be back soon, but after a while those kinds of assurances wouldn't even satisfy a toddler, and Graham was older than either of them.

"I'm sorry," Pod said.

"Let's go up and see if we can spot them," Essie said quietly.

They went up on deck. The moon was up, casting a silver trail across the water.

"I thought this time...," Essie said, but went no further.

"At least they spoke to him," Pod said.

They lapsed into silence, but it was a silence that was quickly broken by another sound. A dinghy was purring up the channel.

"Is that them?" Pod said.

It was too dark to see clearly, but as the dinghy came closer, they could just make out three figures sitting in it.

Essie peered at the occupants, trying to penetrate the darkness through sheer force of will. "Maybe it is them! Maybe they found him after all!"

But as the dinghy came closer to the mouth of the channel, it veered well away from them and steered out toward the open ocean.

"It can't be them," Essie said, disappointed.

Then a surprising thing happened. The dinghy cut its engine and came to a stop. There was a pause. And then the surface of the ocean began to seethe. The water was moving, as if something was stirring down below. It moved and it churned and then lifted and broke, and something came rising up out of the water, something long and metal and gleaming.

It was a submarine.

Essie and Pod looked at it in astonishment. "Is that a pirate submarine?" Essie asked.

"Could be Admiralty," Pod said. "But it seems a bit sneaky for them. Why wouldn't they just do it in plain sight?"

A hatch flipped open in the top of the submarine

and someone stepped out. The dinghy started up again and curved around to stop beside the hatch. One by one, two male passengers got out of the dinghy, climbed up a ladder, stepped into the hatch, and disappeared inside the submarine. The driver of the dinghy passed up two duffel bags, then he waved to the man on the submarine and drove away. The submarine stayed where it was for a few minutes longer while the hatch was locked down, then a horn sounded and the submarine submerged, leaving behind nothing but a swirl of white water that quickly dissipated, leaving no sign that it had ever been there.

Promises

Half an hour later, another dinghy came up the channel. This time they had no difficulty recognizing it.

"So we're going home, then?" Essie said when Will and Annalie had filled them in on the conversation. They were all sitting around the saloon table; it was after midnight.

"Not necessarily," Will said.

"I thought you promised Spinner you would."

"We promised to stay safe," Will said. "We never said anything about going home."

"You really want to keep going?" Pod said.

"To Sundia?" Essie said. "Even though your dad specifically told you not to?"

"Yes," Will said.

"And even though it's impossible to get to Sundia?" Pod said.

"Yes," Will said.

Pod and Essie looked at each other. Then all three of them turned to look at Annalie.

"What do you think?" Essie asked.

Annalie looked back at them for a moment. Then

she said, quietly determined, "I'm in."

Will crowed and gave her a high five, then collected himself slightly as he turned back to Essie and Pod.

"You guys really don't have to come any farther," he began. "If you want—"

"It's all right," Essie said. "I'm coming."

Will turned to Pod. "What about you?"

Pod shrugged. "Where else am I going to go?"

Will jumped up. "Okay, that's settled then. Sundia, here we come!"

In fall 2019, Mardi McConnochie's epic cli-fi trilogy will reach its thrilling conclusion. Set sail for *The Skeleton Coast*.

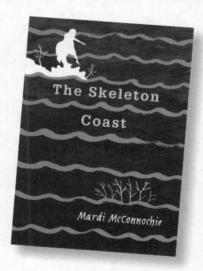

The crew of the *Sunfish*, pursued by the relentless Admiralty, must now brave the treacherous Outer Ocean on their journey to Sundia. This isolated country, forbidden to outsiders, is where the friends must make their final stand in their quest for answers—and for Spinner.